# BACK TO THE INQUISITION

## LOVE THROUGHOUT TIME
### BOOK SIX

## ID JOHNSON

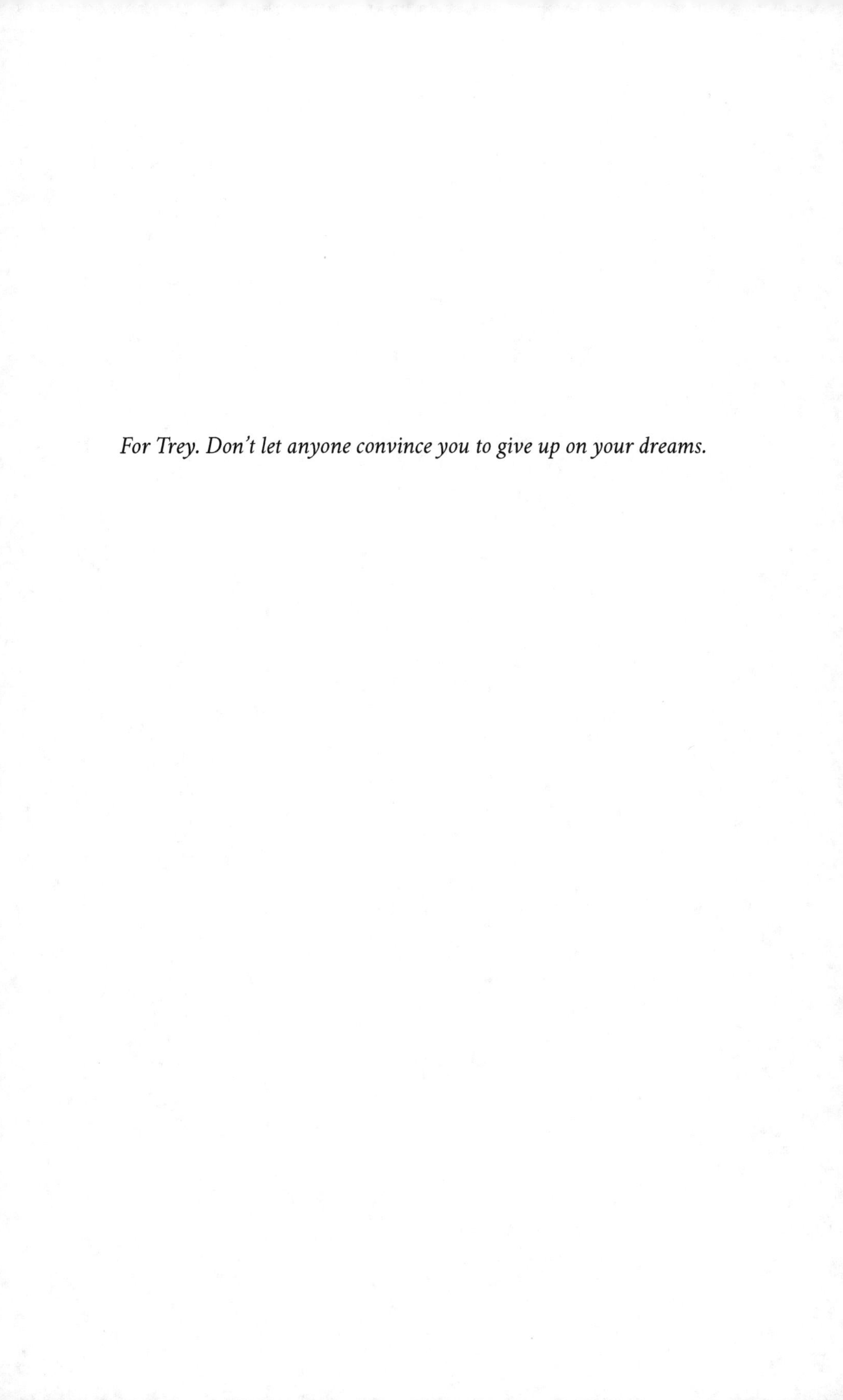

*For Trey. Don't let anyone convince you to give up on your dreams.*

# CONTENTS

1

# LOVE RULED BY TIME

*Ava*

The parking lot is already half full when I pull in, gravel crunching beneath the tires. I sit for a moment with my hands on the wheel, watching a group of teenagers in cloaks laugh their way toward the front gates. One has a plastic sword, another wears elf ears.

I exhale slowly, then shut off the engine and open the door. Walking around to the trunk, I pull out the boxes of supplies for my booth, carrying the familiar, quiet ache with me, though I hadn't expected it would ruin my fun today.

The wind catches my hair as I make my way up the path. Somewhere in the distance, a lute plays a lilting tune, and the smell of roasted meat mingles with the crisp bite of early autumn. My boots sink into the soft earth as I pass beneath the arched wooden sign, *Ye Olde Renaissance.*

The festival grounds open before me in a burst of color, with banners snapping overhead, skirts swishing, and voices calling out in mock accents. It should feel like magic.

It used to....

Last year, Patrick bought us matching tankards, and he'd narrate everything in a fake British accent, challenging strangers to duels. I

1

loved that about him, how easily he could play, but now, the memory stings.

I nod politely at a juggler and smile at a small girl in fairy wings, but I can't quite lose the heaviness. We dated for four years, long enough to think it would last, but then his best friend introduced him to a twenty-two-year-old cocktail waitress, and just like that, he broke up with me. The heartbreak is still a fresh wound, one I keep trying to outpace.

I remind myself that I didn't come here to sulk over a breakup, even if it's only been a week and a half. I came for history, language, and to share my research.

The Iberian Renaissance booth sits near the edge of the artisan quarter, nestled between the mapmaker and the apothecary. It wasn't always here. When I first started coming to the festival as a child, there wasn't an Iberian corner at all. But now, I'm a professor of Iberian studies and a lifelong lover of all things Ren Fest, so five years ago I asked if I could set up a booth to share the heritage I'm proud of, the rich blend of cultures that shaped the Iberian Peninsula during the Renaissance. Since then, it's become one of the festival's best-loved spots, drawing curious visitors eager to learn about the art, language, and history of Spain and Portugal.

A weathered canvas sign overhead reads *España del Renacimiento*, painted in rich crimson and gold. I smooth the edge of the embroidered tablecloth and adjust the display of replica artifacts: a small astrolabe, a miniature of the Alhambra, hand-bound facsimiles of illuminated manuscripts, and a pair of castanets. The tapestry backdrop glows warm in the sun, patterned with the lion and castle of Castile and León.

For the first hour, I keep myself busy. I speak with a high school teacher planning a world history unit. I answer a little girl's question about the princess in one of my paintings, explaining it's actually Queen Isabella, who was not a perfect figure, I admit, but powerful and complicated.

A teenage girl brushes a strand of hair behind her ear while reading a display of ancient Spanish parchments, and asks, "Did people really speak Spanish like that back then? It looks so different."

I smile. "Yes, it changed a lot over time. The Spanish of the Renaissance sounded more formal and musical, shaped by the mix of cultures on the Iberian Peninsula. Christians, Jews, and Muslims all lived there and spoke different languages. The Jews spoke Ladino, a kind of old Spanish mixed with Hebrew, and the Muslims spoke Andalusi Arabic. So the Spanish you hear today carries echoes of all of them."

Nearby, a small group of children clusters around, their eyes bright with curiosity. One little boy pipes up, "Is it like how my abuela talks?"

I kneel to his level. "That's a great question. The Spanish you hear from your abuela has some similarities. This is older and full of expressions you might not hear today. The Spanish of the Renaissance was even more formal and flowery. Let me show you."

I speak a few lines from a famous sixteenth-century poem, emphasizing the rhythm and the way the words roll off the tongue differently than modern Spanish. The kids listen, fascinated, trying to repeat the phrases with varying success and lots of laughter.

The teenage girl smiles. "It's like a secret code."

"Exactly," I say, "a language alive with history and stories."

Teaching helps me forget about Patrick for a moment. There's comfort in what I know, centuries of layered belief and beauty, contradiction and culture, all woven in. For a few hours, I almost forget how hollow I've felt since the breakup.

Around midday, I take a break. The festival is at its peak now, with the crowds swelling and music spilling from every corner. I wander toward the fortune-teller's tent, not quite meaning to.

It's different this year, draped in dark velvet, pinned with silver stars and runes. A sign outside reads simply: *Tarot. Fate. Truths Beyond Time.*

I hover for a beat too long, and the woman inside looks up. She's older than I expect, with a narrow face and thick grey hair braided over one shoulder. Her eyes are kind but knowing, in a way that gives me goosebumps on the back of my neck.

"You have questions," she says, not quite a greeting, her voice mysterious. "And you've come a long way to ask them."

I almost laugh. "I just walked over from the history booth."

She smiles like she knows better. "Come. Sit."

Part of me wants to walk away. The other part, the part that's tired of logic, tired of holding myself together, steps forward and sinks onto the cushion across from her.

She deals the cards in silence. The first shows a crown with broken thorns. The second, a burning tower. The third, two figures standing on opposite sides of a river.

I study them, frowning. "That's not exactly cheerful."

"It's not meant to be. You're standing at the threshold of something old. Something new. Something waiting. The fate of a kingdom. Love written by time."

I exhale slowly, trying to brush off the unease creeping into my chest. "This is about *love*?" I ask.

She doesn't blink. "It's about choices. About bloodlines and betrayal. Your fate resting on what's buried and what's yet to be found."

"That's... vague."

"You'll understand," she says, gathering the cards again, "when the past reaches for you. You must decide whether to take its hand." She leans in, her eyes narrow. "You think you came here to tell tales, but *your story* is just beginning, *profesora*."

I'm shocked at the word. She shouldn't know that. It's not written anywhere, not on the booth, and I'm not wearing a badge. I open my mouth, but she's already looking away, motioning to the next guest.

I walk back through the crowd dazed, her words circling like ravens. *The fate of a kingdom. Love ruled by time....*

It's nothing. A well-rehearsed act. Still, I had goosebumps, and somehow she knows I'm a professor. I shake my head as I walk away, telling myself it was just theater and nothing more.

I weave through the festival crowd, letting the rhythm of drums pull me along. Sunlight glints off polished chain mail. A woman in a green velvet gown sings an old ballad near the cider tent, her voice light and airy as a leaf on the breeze. Jugglers mock each other as they toss six flaming swords into the air. A group of children in fox masks race past, shrieking with laughter.

I duck into a stall filled with hand-bound books and herbal sachets, thumbing the edge of a leather journal too expensive to justify. The vendor chats with someone in a pirate coat about sage bundles and moon phases. I pretend to be absorbed in the scent of lavender and cloves, enjoying the anonymity, the simplicity. No emails. No department meetings. But also no Patrick.

I wander past the archery range, pausing to admire a falconer's bird, its dark eyes watchful and still. I always love this part: the blend of spectacle and scholarship. The way the past feels like a costume you can try on and, for a little while, truly believe in.

Somewhere nearby, a lute plays a tune that's lively, yet somehow mournful, the notes twining through the crowd. The scent of roasting meat mingles with kettle corn and sweet fried dough, and it's almost too easy to imagine the paved path beneath my feet turning to dirt, the tents transforming into market stalls, the chatter shifting to old dialects.

A woodcarver lifts a wooden chest, gesturing for a curious customer to inspect it, while a woman spins wool into thread on a small wheel. I pause, taking it all in, letting myself sink into the illusion of another time.

I am just rounding the corner toward the tapestries and embroidery tents when I hear my name, carried by a familiar voice. I freeze for a moment, scanning the crowd, wondering who could have spotted me among all the festival-goers.

"Ava?"

I turn. It's Erin, one of the graduate assistants from the department. She's dressed in a Tudor-style gown, holding a roasted turkey leg in one hand and looking genuinely delighted.

"It's great to see you!" she says, beaming. "Is Patrick here, too?"

The question slices clean through me. I force a smile. "No. Not this time."

"Oh," she says, her expression shifting as she registers my discomfort. "I'm sorry. I didn't—"

"It's fine," I cut in gently. "I'm just here for the celebration. You look wonderful in your gown."

"Thank you! I love going all out for the weekend." She adjusts the angle of her turkey leg, suddenly aware of how awkward it is to eat. "Your gown is so beautiful, too. What is it—early sixteenth century?"

"Late fifteenth, early sixteenth," I say.

"It's gorgeous."

"Thank you. It's my take on something Isabella might have worn."

"Wow. Very cool. Well, I've got to catch up with my boyfriend over at the Robin Hood show, but maybe I'll see you at the closing parade?"

"Of course," I say.

She smiles again. "Bye for now!"

Erin walks off, blending into the crowd. The sounds of the festival close back in around me, and I hear an announcement that the joust is about to begin. For once, I decide to stay and watch it instead of slipping back to my booth.

The stands are full of people clutching root beer and corn dogs, cheering for knights in crested armor. It's a little silly, a lot staged, but still, it thrills something inside me.

Two horses thunder past, their riders lowering lances with practiced flair. The crowd roars when a shield shatters, and I find myself smiling. The dust, the pageantry, the children waving pennants....

It all feels larger than life.

For a few moments, I let myself be part of it. I clap when the red knight takes a bow, and I laugh when the "queen" tosses a fake chicken into the crowd as a jab at the bawdy tongued herald.

After the final pass, I rise with the rest of the spectators and head back toward my booth. The sun is lower now, casting long golden rays across the grass. My feet know the path by heart, past the soap maker, around the falafel stand, near the replica castle that anchors the far end of the fairgrounds.

I slow down as I approach it. The castle's always been one of the more elaborate attractions, its façade meant to evoke medieval stonework, complete with painted battlements and a wooden drawbridge. It's not perfect, but it has presence.

The castle is ringed by a narrow moat, sometimes dry, sometimes filled with a shallow trickle of water, but this year, it's nearly full.

The water is dark, almost black, beneath the shade of overhanging trees. Ripples move lazily across the surface, catching the dying light like liquid glass. I stop at the edge, peering down. I can't even see the bottom.

I wrap my arms across my chest, more thoughtful than cold. It looks deep enough to swim in, I think. Deeper than I remember.

A wind stirs the trees behind me. Somewhere far off, someone sings in Spanish, modern, but with an old melody. It echoes strangely off the stone.

I don't realize how close I'm standing to the edge until a sudden commotion breaks the stillness.

Laughing and shouting, a group of teenagers rush past behind me, all noise, limbs, and foam swords. One of them knocks into my shoulder, hard.

I stumble, slip on the grass, and scream as I fall into the moat. Cold water rushes over me. My head slams against something hard, a rock, maybe.

Pain flares, then everything goes black.

2

## GHOSTS AND THE TAGUS

*LUCA*

THE TAVERN'S dim light glows against the rough-hewn walls as I lean on the worn oak table, the wine warming my chest. Around me, allies and old friends murmur low, their voices heavy with suspicion. They talk in hushed tones about the shifting tides of power.

The Catholic Monarchs are tightening their grip, and there are whispers of Moorish resistance crumbling, and of courtiers scheming beneath gilded masks. Here, politics isn't a game. It's a double-edged sword, and tonight, every word feels like a move in a deadly dance we can't afford to lose.

I keep my face still and my answers careful. Too much depends on silence. My lineage is better left unspoken, a truth buried beneath titles and loyalty pledges.

I swirl the wine in my cup and listen to Ramón, red-faced and angry in the way that always precedes a mistake. He spits out names like curses, blaming everyone from the king's advisors to his own brother for the increasing pressure on Toledo's nobles. He wants a target, a quick solution, but all we have are questions.

"Luca," he says finally, his voice too loud in the quiet. "You've been silent all night. Tell us, what would you do?"

I lift my eyes. "If I were reckless? I'd draw my sword, cut down the tax collectors, and rally everyone from the city to the hills."

A few chuckles. Ramón looks satisfied.

"But I'm not reckless," I add. "Not anymore."

There's silence again. The fire pops in the hearth. I glance around at the men I've known since childhood, men I've bled beside, men who stood at my side when my father fell. They know about the blood I carry, the legacy of a Muslim noble line, spoken of only in whispers. And I know their secrets too, hidden beneath smiles and guarded words. We all carry confidences, because in this city, a single truth revealed could undo us all.

"We've survived betrayal, sieges, starvation… but this feels different. It's not like war. It's a slow death, veiled in laws and proclamations, a careful erasure. They're not coming with swords anymore. This time, they're wearing robes, signing edicts, and smiling as they do it. They're bleeding us quietly," I continue, standing. "Exiling scholars, confiscating homes."

I cross to the window and push it open, needing the cold night air. Beyond the dark rooftops, the palace towers shimmer in the moonlight. For a heartbeat, I remember what it felt like to believe we might win. Before it was obvious the Crown would stop at nothing to destroy my people. Before silence began to feel like the only true safety.

"They're dividing us," someone mutters. "Making us watch each other."

I nod. "And we've let them. Hoping it would pass. That if we bowed our heads long enough, it would be enough."

Ramón finally speaks, his voice hard. "So what now, Luca? We wait for them to knock down our doors? Or do we remind them we're not ghosts yet?"

"They already knock down our doors, Ramón, almost every night. But we can't call for a true rebellion yet," I say. "Right now, all I'm asking for are eyes and ears open. Loyalty where it counts. We don't strike unless we must. We don't give them reasons to lock us up."

A few murmurs rise in agreement. No cheers or toasts, just a shared, uneasy understanding. Ramón leans back, his arms crossed, but he doesn't argue any more tonight.

The fire has burned low. I pull my cloak over my shoulders and step toward the door.

Tomas raises an eyebrow. "Off already?"

"I've said what I came to say."

I nod once and then push open the door, stepping out into the narrow alley behind the tavern, the wind sharp against my face. Below, the waters of the Tagus River gleam in the beams of the moon, winding eastward.

I walk with no real destination, past shuttered windows and quiet homes, beyond the edge of Plaza de Zocodover, where covered market stalls stand empty and the square sleeps under a heavy stillness.

I pass the chapel steps beside the towering walls of the Castillo de San Servando and pause for a breath, enveloped by the scent of blooming orange blossoms and fresh herbs, vibrant signs of spring in Toledo. I gaze up at the fortress's towers, rising pale and watchful against the stars. Somewhere behind those walls, men in velvet robes draft new decrees by candlelight, and someone sharpens a quill like a blade.

*Let them. We're not ghosts yet.*

I pull my hood higher and turn toward the road that skirts the river's edge. Dawn is just beginning to stretch her fingers over the rooftops, bathing the city in a pale blue. A black cat slips across a shadowed alley. The bell tolls, its steady chime threading through the city, beckoning Toledo to wake and rise.

My boots slide on the dew-slick cobblestones of the bridge, the harsh bite of morning air sharpening my senses, clearing the fog of wine from my mind.

The Tagus is dark and still beneath the new dawn. Slowly, something in the water drifts toward the stone bridge, carried by the gentle current. At first, I can't make out what it is, but as it floats closer, I see hair fanning out like ink just beneath the surface. Shocked, I realize that it's a limp body, lying still and motionless, face down in the water.

Without hesitation, I throw off my cloak and plunge in, boots and all. The water bites sharp and freezing through my clothes, but adrenaline pushes me forward. She slips beneath again, cold and heavy, but my fingers find her wrist. I grip tight and pull her close. Suddenly, she stirs, a weak cough bubbling up as I drag us toward the embankment.

With muscles burning, I shove her onto the shore first. She collapses with a choking sob, coughing and gasping for air. I haul myself out after her, panting, soaked, and trembling from the cold.

We sit there in silence, our breaths ragged, the Tagus lapping quietly behind us. Our breath curls in the crisp morning air like smoke.

She turns her head slowly toward me. Her eyes are deep blue, rimmed red. Her lips tremble, but it's not just the cold. She looks dazed, and perhaps lost.

"Are you hurt?" I ask.

She doesn't answer, just stares at me like she doesn't understand the words.

"Who are you?" I try again, softer now. "Can you speak?"

Still nothing, but she looks down at my wet tunic, then at the towers beyond me, like she's remembering something, or deciding how to.

"I…." Her voice is hoarse, ragged. "I don't know where I am."

I frown. "You're in Toledo. Near the fortress walls."

She glances around again, hesitating. "Toledo… in Spain?"

I shake my head, utterly confused. "No. Castilla."

Her accent is strange with flattened vowels, and an odd rhythm, like she learned it far from here, and she called this place *Spain*.

I watch her closely. "Where did you say you came from?"

Her lips part like she's about to say something, then she shuts them again. Whatever confusion she's wrestling with, she doesn't want to share it yet.

"I thought you'd drowned," I mutter, wringing the water from my tunic. "What were you doing?"

She wraps her arms around herself. "I—I fell. There were people. And then…."

Her voice drifts off. She's shaking now, the wet fabric plastered to her skin, her teeth chattering. Even drenched, the gown clinging to her is fine, richer than anything I've ever seen, the kind of silk and embroidery only a queen would wear. Something Isabella herself might favor. She must be a noblewoman.

I offer her my dry cloak and wrap it around her shoulders. She flinches at my touch but doesn't pull away. Her eyes are glassy, unfocused, as though she's taken a blow to the head.

I should walk away and let the guards deal with her. I don't need the trouble. A soaked, trembling noblewoman with a thousand unspoken questions is more than I bargained for.

Still, I stay.

She's staring down at her lap now. "I can't seem to remember," she says quietly. "Who I am. Just… bits and pieces."

Her voice is ragged with uncertainty. The words she chooses catch me off guard. Some are unfamiliar, as if she's pieced them together from different times and places. Some don't belong here.

There's no reason to help her, certainly none that makes sense. Yet I find myself saying, "I know someone. Someone who might be able to help."

She lifts her eyes to mine, wary and searching.

"I'm Luca."

A pause, then a whisper: "Ava."

I steady her as she rises, the wet gown clinging to a slender form with curves like an hour glass. She moves with unexpected grace. Her long dark hair is damp and tangled, and her vivid blue eyes catch the morning light like something otherworldly—eyes so rare, they hold me still for a heartbeat.

Side by side, we step forward, walking slowly into the soft glow of Toledo's spring morning.

3

# COMA DREAM

## *AVA*

MY LUNGS BURN as the chilled air fills them, each breath sharp and shallow. Luca's hand slips from my arm, but I stay close, unsure where else to go.

A dull ache throbs in my head, blurring everything around me. The town is just waking. A few early risers pause and stare as we pass, our soaked cloaks dripping onto the stones, strange in this quiet dawn. Their eyes narrow, curiosity flickering alongside suspicion. I feel exposed, like a creature caught far from its home.

The language drifting around me sounds like the Castilian I studied with its flowery, older words and phrases. It's as if the language has held onto its ancient form here, a living relic. Why would anyone still speak like this? The question tugs at me as we walk.

The scent of damp earth and river water clings to the air, mingling with the faint aroma of blooming orange blossoms. The castle in the distance, its turrets rising like jagged teeth into the dawn, looks just like the ones I've seen in old paintings of Toledo, the kind hung in dusty museums or buried in the pages of my art history textbooks.

It doesn't make sense. None of it does.

I remember slipping, the sudden cold of the moat at the Renaissance Festival, the sharp crack of my head against something hard, and then this—the worn stone streets and ancient language. Maybe I'm still unconscious, my mind flinging me deeper into some vivid dream.

I force my voice steady. "I think I hit my head," I say, hesitating. "I don't know who I am." The words feel strange coming from me, like a dishonest confession in a language that doesn't sound quite right.

Luca's brow furrows, but he says nothing. He only nods once and tightens his hold on my hand. We move through narrow, twisting streets paved with uneven stone, walls rising like silent sentinels on either side.

Dawn paints the sky in pale blues and soft pinks. The city slowly stirs. Few people are out. I catch cautious glances from windows or a merchant setting up wares in the market square. Eyes linger on us, both soaked and shivering.

Finally, we reach a small, sturdy home set back from the main street. Luca knocks, and a kind-faced woman opens the door, her eyes soft and full of quiet concern. She greets him warmly in the same ancient Spanish and casts a long look at me, drenched, disheveled, and clearly out of place. Still, she doesn't hesitate. With a quiet nod, she steps aside and gestures us inside.

The home is simple but clean, with low wooden beams and the strong scent of herbs and wood smoke lingering in the air. She leads me to a small room, rummages through a stack of neatly folded clothes, and hands me a plain wool dress. Without a word, she steps outside and closes the door behind her, leaving me the privacy to change.

I peel off the soaked silk, what's left of my gown, and step into the rough-spun fabric. It scratches at my skin, unfamiliar, but it's dry, warm, and for now, that's enough.

When I emerge, Luca stands near the hearth, his arms crossed, his dark hair still wet and curling at the ends. He looks up, and something shifts in his eyes when he sees me. Not surprise exactly. Maybe relief. Maybe curiosity.

Luca nods. "Rest," he says simply. "I'll come back later to check on you." Then he turns and slips out the door, the latch clicking softly shut behind him.

The woman settles me in with the warm meal, her kindness a comfort to the turmoil inside. I try to focus on the rich, simple broth, the way it soothes my burning throat and warms my chilled body, but my thoughts spin, confusion twisting tighter.

*Where the hell am I?*

The question coils deep in my chest. I know exactly who I am, but the world around me is too ancient, too real—these narrow stone streets, the flicker of iron lamps, the air scented with wood smoke and livestock.

The old woman bustles around the small kitchen, her movements sure and practiced. The fire crackles low in the hearth, casting shadows on the stone walls. She sets a second bowl of broth before me, steam floating up in fragrant wisps.

"Eat, niña," she says, her voice gentle. "It's been a long night."

I nod, hesitant, my throat tight. "Thank you... I'm Ava."

She pauses, then offers a small smile. "They call me Abuela María. You rest now, Ava. The world outside is not kind to those who are lost."

I wrap my hands around the bowl, savoring the warmth. The fabric of the dress is rough against my skin. The woman's kindness is meek and quiet—no questions, no suspicion. Just care.

"Thank you," I murmur.

She nods and sits across from me with a tired sigh, folding a piece of cloth in her lap. "Strange days," she says, half to herself. "Death, disappearances... every one of us feels uneasy."

I glance up at her, my heart ticking faster. Her macabre words chill me more than the river did.

She catches my look and offers a faint smile. "Just... be careful, child. People look twice at those they don't recognize. These are not times for standing out."

A cold thread winds through my chest. I lower my gaze to the bowl and take a cautious sip. Despite the warmth, I feel the chill of her warning settle deep in my bones.

My thoughts keep drifting back to Luca. The way his jaw holds the faint shadow of stubble, the way he watched me like he could see through the fog inside me. There's something about him I can't shake. I'm not sure if I trust him, but I'm glad he found me. Glad he spoke a language I understood, even if it sounds like something torn from an etymology book.

The Spanish here is archaic, the rhythm unfamiliar, but I catch the meaning. Thank God I studied it obsessively, and not just for fun. I wrote my thesis on the evolution of Iberian dialects, dissected the syntax of royal decrees and secret messages, and letters from the ancient century that is far too like my current surroundings.

What once felt academic now feels like survival. Without it, I wouldn't even know how to say thank you.

The realization that I didn't thank Luca hits too late. I was too dazed, too shaken, too consumed by the strangeness of it all. He helped me, rescued me, and I let him leave without a word of thanks. I hope I get the chance to say it. I hope I see Luca again.

I told him I don't remember who I am. I said I hit my head. It's a lie I'll need to stick to until I can come up with something better, because the truth is I don't know how I got here. I don't know what year it is, but I know this isn't my world, and I want to go back.

I want to go back to Patrick, to the apartment we shared, the record player in the corner, the soft way he'd say my name. I ache for the normalcy of it all, for the little things I never thought I'd lose.

I wonder if my family knows I'm gone. If my sister Eden is pacing some sterile hallway, demanding answers. If my parents are sitting next to a hospital bed that still holds my body, holding onto hope. I picture them there, waiting. For what, I don't know.

Abuela Maria offers me a blanket and leads me back to the small room where I changed earlier. She gestures to the narrow bed in the corner, the linens rough textured but clean. I murmur my thanks as I sit, and she gives a small nod then steps out quietly, leaving me alone with the hum of her soft, wordless tune lingering behind her.

Before lying down, I pick up the gown I'd worn, once so breathtaking, now soaked and heavy in my hands. The silk is still cool, clinging in places where it hasn't yet dried. Gold embroidery shimmers faintly along the ebony sleeves, threads catching the firelight like they're trying to pretend none of this ever happened. But the hem is torn, muddied from the struggle, and there's a long rip along the side seam I hadn't noticed before. I smooth it out gently and lay it across the chair by the wall, the ruined elegance of it making something tighten in my chest. Like I've left a piece of myself behind on a battlefield I never meant to walk into.

I lie back against the lumpy mattress and stare up at the cracks in the ceiling. Nothing about this place makes sense. Not the way the broth tasted real, not the heaviness of the clothes, not the sting of the cold river still lingering in my bones.

I remember Ren Fest. The laughter, the music, the rowdy teenagers, and the muddy edge of the moat. I slipped and hit my head. That's what this has to be. A dream. A coma. Some fevered hallucination while doctors hover over my body and my name is being whispered by people I love. Or maybe I died. Maybe this is the in-between.

Whatever it is, it isn't real life. It can't be.

4

___

# ORDER TO CHAOS

## *LUCA*

THE WARM SCENT of fresh cheese and sweet figs fills the tavern. I break off a piece of crusty bread and drizzle it with thick honey, savoring the sharp contrast. A small bowl of olives sits nearby, salty against the sweetness. Around me, the tavern hums with mid-morning bustle—merchants counting coins, farmers swapping news, and the barkeep wiping down the tables.

I'm glad I managed to change out of my drenched clothes hours ago. Although sleep has evaded me, at least my belly is full. I hadn't meant to stop for a noblewoman, dazed and soaked to the bone, speaking Castilian like it was borrowed from another tongue. She should've been someone else's problem, but I pulled her out anyway, wrapped her in my cloak, and took her to Abuela Maria's home just as the sun came up. A foolish risk, and yet, it had to be done. I couldn't just leave her there.

I chew slowly, scanning the street through the window. Right on time, the boy appears—dirty knees, hollow cheeks, a basket of herbs slung over one shoulder. He doesn't glance my way. He just enters the tavern, loops past my table, and lets something slip beneath the bench as he stumbles.

I wait five breaths before retrieving the folded scrap of parchment. Plain seal. No names.

*They're moving early. The warrant's been signed.*

*Three households marked.*

I exhale through my nose and slide the note into my boot. They're getting bolder.

The palace gleams in the distance, smug and golden. Once, I would've walked those halls without fear. Once, my name would've protected me, but that was before my father refused to burn our holy books. Before my mother taught my younger sisters how to read. Before we became traitors.

I pay my tab and step out of the tavern. I should be heading in any direction but this one. There are warnings to deliver, quiet deals waiting to be struck, but my steps turn toward Abuela María's small house all the same.

Maybe it's the bruise on the woman's temple I can't get out of my mind, or the way her soaked gown fit for a queen clung to her curves in the sunlight.

Maybe it's the way her voice sounded odd, or how she looked like someone rich who'd been dragged through the gutter, and even then, even dazed and half-drowned, there was something about her that pulled at me. Not just her beauty, though I'd be lying if I said it didn't catch me off guard. There's a gravity to her.

She might be dangerous. She might be someone's pawn, or some-one's prize, but I pulled her out of the water, and I'm the one who dropped her at María's door. If she turns out to be trouble, it should be *my* eyes that catch it first.

The door to Abuela María's house groans as I knock once, announce myself, and ease it open. She doesn't look up from her dough, just keeps kneading with slow, practiced motions. The scent of warm bread, garlic, and wood smoke fills the tiny kitchen.

"She's awake," María says, dusting her hands on her apron. "She said her head still hurts, but she took broth and half a fig. That's something."

I nod. "Thank you for helping her, Abuela. Do you mind if I check on her?"

María gestures toward the back room without looking at me. "Don't spook her. She's still floating between here and nowhere."

Maria always talks like that, half prayer, half warning. She isn't my *real* grandmother, not by blood, but she's patched up every lost soul in this quarter for twenty years, including me.

The back room is dim and quiet. A single candle burns on the windowsill. Ava sits on the bed with her back straight, a blanket wrapped around her shoulders and dark curls framing her pretty face. The bruising on her temple has faded to a sickly yellow, but she's beautiful all the same with those eyes that shine like sapphires.

She looks up at me as I step in. "You came back," she says.

"I wanted to see how you were doing."

Her hand rises to her temple. "I just have a headache. It feels like someone cracked a melon over my head."

I chuckle. "That sounds about right."

Ava doesn't smile. She looks tired but alert, and there's no panic in her voice, no noble outrage at the modest room or the common blanket tucked around her.

"Do you remember anything yet?" I ask.

She shakes her head slowly. "No. Just that my name is Ava. Everything before the water is a blank."

"Any idea where you were going? Or coming from?"

"No." She glances down at her lap. "It's like waking up in someone else's life."

There's no fear in her tone. No performance, either. She speaks plainly, as if she's already turned this over a dozen times in her mind and found nothing new. Most nobles would be weeping or demanding a physician, but Ava just sits there calmly.

"You're lucky you didn't drown," I say. "I mean, I don't know how you didn't drown. I thought I was pulling a dead body from the river."

She pauses, then shifts slightly on the bed. "I forgot to thank you," she says, more serious than I expected. "For pulling me out. For not leaving me there." Her voice is quiet but sincere. "That was kindness I didn't earn."

I glance at her, caught off guard. I've heard gratitude before, but not like that. Not so plain and direct, like it actually cost her something to say it.

Her eyes catch the light, strikingly blue against the dark curls that tumble around her face and the warm olive tone of her skin. It's a combination I've never seen before, and for a moment, I'm pulled away from the weight I carry, distracted by the quiet mystery she holds in her beauty. She's a puzzle, a story I don't yet know, and more than that a glimpse of something worth the curiosity and wonderment in a life full of shadows.

"You're most welcome, but I think you should know," I say. "If anyone starts asking questions, I'll hear about it."

"Should I be worried?"

I shrug. "Depends on who you are."

"Well," she says softly, "I'll let you know if I find out."

I nod once. There's nothing more to say, not right now. I turn toward the door, but I pause in the frame.

"Would you like to get some fresh air?" I ask without looking back. "It might help clear your head."

She hesitates only a moment before rising. "Yes," she says softly. "Thank you. I think I'd like that."

I offer her my arm, and she takes it, lightly, like she's not used to leaning on anyone. We step outside, and I call back to Abuela María, "We'll be back soon."

She waves us off without turning from her bread.

As we walk toward the plaza, I watch Ava out of the corner of my eye. The way her gaze catches on the tiled rooftops, the laundry lines, the vendors shouting their morning prices—every reaction is a clue. Every silence, a question. I intend to find the answers.

She squints at the sunlight. "I think the fresh air is helping already."

I keep my tone light, easy. Let her believe I'm being kind. In truth,

I want her out in the open, to see how she reacts, who or what she notices, and whether anyone recognizes her.

She doesn't ask where we're going. She just walks beside me, her eyes absorbing every corner of the city like she's seeing it for the first time. Maybe she is.

We pass the cathedral, its twin towers stabbing the sky. A group of brown-cloaked priests stands by the entrance, whispering with a cluster of guards. Ava's gaze lingers there a moment too long.

"You're very quiet," I say.

"I'm sorry, I don't mean to be rude. I'm just lost in my own thoughts."

"Oh? If I may be so bold, what are you thinking about?"

Her fingers tighten slightly on my arm. "How strange it feels to not *truly recognize* a place that looks so familiar."

I nod as if I understand. I don't, but I *do* know how to listen.

We move past the butcher's row and down toward the market stalls. The morning crowd has thinned, but soldiers and guards still drift between booths like wolves circling. We keep our distance.

Ava notices. I can tell by the shift in her posture.

"They've increased patrols lately," I say.

"Are they looking for someone in particular?"

"Always."

We pause at the edge of the square, where a young girl sells almonds wrapped in paper cones. I buy two, hand Ava one, and lead us toward the stone bench beneath the fig tree.

Only once we're seated do I say, "They say King Ferdinand and Queen Isabella have brought order to chaos."

Ava stiffens beside me. Her gaze lifts toward the cathedral spires, then the soldiers posted near the fountain. A darkness passes over her face, something like realization, as though he's seeing the world around her clearly for the first time.

I study her quietly. She *did* hit her head. Maybe this is it. Maybe the fog is finally lifting, and she's remembering who she is. Then she speaks.

"Is that what they call it? Order to chaos?" Her voice is sharper now.

I glance sideways, feigning disinterest. "Do you disagree?"

"Yes," she says flatly. "I do. Order built on fear isn't order. It's control. They burn religious scripts. Drive out anyone who doesn't fit their vision. That's not peace. That's cultural execution."

Her words surprise me. Not just their truth, but the bluntness of them. It's the kind of thing no one says aloud, especially not near the cathedral, not unless they want to disappear by nightfall. And yet, I completely agree with her. It's rare to find someone who sees it so clearly. Rarer still in a woman who was dressed like a noble.

She speaks like a rebel. So why did I find her in silk?

I nod once, slowly. "Interesting perspective."

"That's a polite way of saying I should be quiet."

"No," I say. "It's a polite way of saying I'm listening."

I say nothing else yet. She doesn't need to know what side I'm on. Not until I know for certain where she stands. The network is already stretched thin. Too many faces, too many secrets, and lately, too many questions.

We've lost three couriers in the last two weeks. One was caught at the south checkpoint with a coded letter sewn into her hem. Another never showed for the drop. The last one, Andre, died with a knife in his side and no message in his pocket. There's a leak, a traitor, and whoever it is, they're smart and careful. Just helping the guards enough to avoid suspicion.

All day, I watch her closely, searching for any sign of recognition when she glimpses a familiar face or hears a name whispered, but no one seems to know her, and she doesn't know anyone. She moves through the city like a shadow among strangers, and I can relate.

Hours have slipped by since we left Abuela María's house, and my stomach growls louder than I care to admit.

"The sun's starting to dip," I say, standing and offering Ava my arm. "Maria's cooking won't wait forever."

The simple hearth, well-worn wooden table, and the steady rhythm of Abuela María's hands serving bowls of stew feel nostalgic, bringing me comfort much like my childhood home. For a moment, I let myself be distracted by the warmth of the kitchen and Ava's quiet presence beside me.

But then I think of the folded note inside my boot. Three households marked, and the signed warrants. The Crown is tightening its grip faster than ever before, since the fall of Granada. My thoughts snap back to the danger waiting outside these walls.

I hate what they're doing, silencing anyone who dares to stand against them. Saving those families is the only thing that matters. I have to warn them. I have to act.

Still, despite everything, Ava's face and voice linger at the edge of my thoughts. There's something about her, something I can't explain, that makes me want to stay a little longer, to learn more. I shove the distraction aside and force myself to eat quickly.

There's work to be done tonight, and I can't afford to waste any time.

5

# EARNING TRUST

## *AVA*

CHURCH BELLS PULL me from a restless sleep. The stone walls of
Abuela Maria's house seem to close in around me as I lie in this
borrowed bed, and still, I tell myself: this has to be a coma dream.

Yesterday, when Luca said Isabella and Ferdinand were king and
queen, it hit me like a blow. I don't belong here, and I keep hoping to
wake up, to open my eyes and find myself at home, or at the very
least, in a hospital bed in my own time.

For days, Luca guides me, always with a watchful eye, through
Toledo's back alleys and tucked-away taverns. We find ways to shop
at certain vendors in the Plaza de Zocodover, keeping to ourselves
through clouds of spice and charcoal smoke.

I recognize the square from illustrations in my lectures, but the
smell of roasting lamb and tallow is raw and real. Children dart
between mule carts. Soldiers in polished morions drift at the edges
like iron shadows. Every time they pass, conversations drop to
whispers.

From there we climb the steep lanes toward the Alcázar, its half-
rebuilt ramparts casting long, noon-bright spears of light. I never
approved of Isabella's methods, but now I feel a deeper, visceral

hatred for what she has built. From the safety of textbooks, I debated her policies and called them "calculated yet cruel." Now, I watch a line of shackled men being marched through the Puerta del Sol and wonder how many will see tomorrow's dawn. Luca doesn't go near the guards. He lingers in narrow alleys, guiding me by back routes, always watching the corners.

Luca pauses at the Monasterio de San Juan de los Reyes, its high stone walls crowned with iron chains that clink faintly in the breeze. "They say the monarchs vowed this place to God after Granada fell," he murmurs, watching me too carefully.

I glance up at the iron shackles and say quietly, "They want people to feel powerless. That's what this is. Not just a celebration, but a warning."

Luca looks shocked. "You speak like someone who's seen it before."

"In a way, I have." I keep my voice even. "It's always the same. Fear dressed up as faith. Piety twisted into power."

He studies me for a moment. "You're not from here, are you?"

My heart lurches. "I told you, I don't remember where I'm from. Perhaps I'm from a mix of places. Let's just say I know what happens when kings confuse God with themselves."

That earns me the faintest smile, a strong contrast on Luca's handsome face, which is usually deep and brooding. "There's a gathering tonight, and you should be there. You truly see this place for what it is… I'll take you."

We cross the stone arch of San Martin Bridge at dusk. The Tagus below glitters copper, gulls skimming its surface. Patrick would love this view. He always chased sunsets for his sketchbook. The ache of missing him cuts deeper than the cool river air. If I could just wake up, if I could just hear him laugh, this nightmare would dissolve like fog.

Luca doesn't tell me where we're going, only that it's a secret meeting and that I should keep my hood up and stay close. I follow him through the crooked alleys of Toledo, past closed-up shops and windows with glowing candles behind their latticework. He walks like someone who's always listening behind him.

The building is low and narrow, wedged between two others like it's hiding. He knocks twice, then once again. There's a pause, a whisper through the crack, and then the door opens just wide enough for us to slip inside.

It's warmer in here. Oil lamps cast golden pools across packed earth and plaster walls. There are maybe fifteen people, mostly men in dark robes, their sandals dusty, their eyes alert.

There are a couple of women, too, and one of them meets my gaze briefly. The moment we enter, faces turn toward us, toward *me*.

Luca lifts a hand. "This is Ava. She's under my protection."

He doesn't say more than that. No explanation of where I'm from or what I'm doing here. Just a firm statement, quiet but absolute. *Under my protection.* And somehow, that's enough. No one welcomes me, but no one objects, either. A few nod. Others glance away and return to their seats. The silence doesn't warm, but it thaws just enough.

We settle near the back, half in shadow. The conversation begins quickly, no further introductions.

"And they've seized the manuscripts from the zawiya near Puerta Nueva."

"That's the third this month. They won't stop at libraries."

"Not now that the Santo Oficio has dug in."

There's a pause. A few men cross themselves reflexively. A woman's voice cuts in, low and clear. "Granada has fallen. They won't be satisfied until every mosque is rubble."

Someone asks, "Have they made the expulsion decree official yet?"

"Not quite—still waiting on the formal order, but it's certain. They'll force conversions or drive us from the kingdom soon enough."

They say "us" like it means one people, but I'm not one of them. Still, I'm with them now, and if this is real, if I'm not just dreaming, I'm caught in something dangerous, something that could destroy everyone in this room.

An elderly man speaks next, his voice heavy with fatigue. "We need new routes out. The northern passage is blocked."

A younger man beside him nods. "Then we go east to Valencia. Or Naples, if it comes to that."

"And Luca?" the older man turns to him, his voice low but steady. Everyone quiets, waiting.

Luca meets the man's gaze, then darts his eyes to the worn floor beneath them. "I had hoped I wouldn't have to leave," he says quietly, "that I would still be here to care for those who cannot leave, like Abuela María, tending to the lost and the broken."

He swallows hard and looks up, rising as he speaks. "I dreamt I could stay forever, help those who have no coin or strength to flee, the sick, the elderly. But–" His voice falters for a moment. "I'm not so sure anymore. It's breaking my heart to say it, but I think we'll all have to go… or be crushed beneath their heel, and that is something I hate with every breath."

I feel something in my chest tighten, an admiration I didn't expect. Luca isn't just a guide or a messenger in this place. He's loyal, brave, and fiercely tied to his people.

The older man nods solemnly. "We must be ready for anything."

Slowly, the murmurs rise again. The meeting breaks up, hands shake, and the small group begins to disperse into the night, melting into the shadows of Toledo's winding streets.

I follow Luca closely, caught between the ache of this brutal reality and the strange comfort of being near someone so steadfast.

The streets are quiet again by the time we leave the meeting house. The lamps are burning low, and even the stray cats have disappeared into the alleys. Luca walks beside me, not saying much, but I can feel the tension in his stride.

"I'm truly grateful you're walking me back," I say softly, the cobblestones muffling our footsteps as we move through the quiet streets. "It means more than I can say."

Luca glances at me with warmth in his eyes. "I'm glad to," he replies simply. "It's the least I can do."

We fall into silence for a moment before I gather the courage to ask, "Why did you invite me to that meeting?"

He looks ahead, thoughtful. "It was your opinion of the Crown. How you see what they're doing. Even if you don't remember who you are, you're a good person."

I swallow hard, surprise and relief flooding me. "I didn't know saying the truth could mean so much."

He chuckles quietly. "The truth can be dangerous around here, but it's also the only thing worth living for."

I pull my hood up even though no one's around. It feels safer, even if nothing about this situation is truly safe.

"What was that back there?" I ask. "A resistance group?"

He hesitates, then nods. "Of a kind."

"And you trust all of them?"

"No, but I trust most of them not to betray the others." He looks at me again. "That's a start."

I glance up at him, curious. "Do you ever worry it's not enough? That trust can break?"

He shrugs, tension tightening his jaw. "I consider it every day, but fear breaks people faster than betrayal. We hold on to what and whom we can."

I nod slowly, feeling his words settle over me. "I'm not sure I understand all of it yet. The risks, and the politics."

Luca's eyes meet mine. "No one can understand all of it. The laws are written in shadows of greed and shame. That's why we watch over each other, and protect each other in silence."

We walk a little farther, and I tuck a loose curl behind my ear, trying to steady my voice. "Do you think things will get better in Toledo?"

He exhales, the sound rough. "I want to believe they will, but right now, survival feels like victory."

The scent of wood smoke grows stronger as we near Abuela María's door. I hesitate, reluctant to break the fragile connection between us.

"Thank you," I say again, softer this time. "For not just saving me, but for trusting me."

Luca offers a faint smile, the first real one I've seen from him tonight. "You earned the trust I've given you so far."

I smile up at Luca as he opens the creaky front door. "Goodnight, Luca."

"Goodnight, Ava," he says as he slips away into the dark city streets again.

I close the door behind me, the sound muffled by the thick stone walls. The house is quiet. Abuela María has already gone to bed.

As I settle into my small, borrowed room, my mind won't stop spinning. The danger, the secrets, the way trust feels like a currency I don't know how to spend, and even though part of me is starting to understand what's at stake here, the truth is I don't belong in this time. I need to get back to 2025. Back to my life, my family, and back to Patrick.

I miss the way he could always make me laugh even on the worst days. His easy grin that somehow made everything feel a little less heavy. I know we broke up just a couple weeks ago, but right now, as I lie here hurting and confused, part of me can't help but imagine he's by my side, sitting quietly in the hospital room, holding my hand until I wake up. I tell myself that when I open my eyes, when this nightmare ends, we'll find our way back to each other. That the distance between us isn't gone, but it's not permanent either.

I miss my parents. Just knowing they're out there, worrying, breaks my heart. And my sister Eden…. I keep thinking about what she'd say if she were here with me right now. She'd roll her eyes and tell me to stop being so dramatic, even though she'd secretly be terrified.

I miss my phone, my apartment, the small comforts of modern life, like running water, the warmth of a shower, the convenience of electricity. Here, surrounded by stone and shadows, those things feel like another lifetime.

And yet, I keep thinking about the way Luca looked at me. The way he trusted me enough to let me attend his meeting. The way he listens....

*This has to be a dream,* I tell myself. *I hit my head, and now I'm in a coma, and this is just my brain pulling images from my papers and studies, Isabella and Ferdinand, the Inquisition. It makes sense. Sort of. Doesn't it?*

I stare at the ceiling, my thoughts swirling.

Eventually, sleep finds me.

6

---

# NOBLE TO REBEL

## *LUCA*

ABUELA MARÍA'S kitchen is warm and quiet, the evening light fading through the small window above the sink. She made dinner earlier, and now Ava and I stand side by side, drying dishes together after cleaning off the table.

Ava is unlike anyone I've ever known. It isn't just her opinions–bold, unflinching thoughts on the court and the men who twist the law to justify slaughter–but there's also the way she speaks of power with fury that suggests she's seen behind the curtain. Ava always seems to know what will happen next. Her guesses land too close to truth, subtle but unsettling. She says she can't remember who she is or where she's from, and perhaps that's true. Even so, she remains an enigma. I find myself drawn to her, but I also don't *fully* trust her yet.

She speaks of Isabella and Ferdinand with a strange fire, unafraid to name their cruelty, to question their decrees, even here, in the heart of their kingdom. It's incredibly dangerous, and yet, her conviction runs deeper than fear, as if the suffering of the people they silence is her own.

Alas, when I ask where she's from, she slips away behind half-answers and shrugs. Her olive skin suggests the south, but her eyes are the pale blue of the north, and her hair—dark and curling like a

37

sea-wind from Italy or Greece, defies any one origin. She doesn't quite fit anywhere, and maybe that's why I can't look away.

My frustration swells. *Who is she really? What truth is she hiding beneath that innocent exterior?* And yet, beneath the frustration, there's a pull, a curiosity I can't shake.

"You speak as if you've seen their courts from the inside," I say quietly. "You know things others don't. How?"

She exhales slowly, finally meeting my eyes. "I'm no spy, if that's what you're worried about," she says, her voice guarded.

Her mystery stretches, heavy and taut. I want to believe her, but in these times, trust is a currency few can afford. I make a quick decision. Maybe if I show her a sliver of my own truth, she'll offer something about herself in return.

"My family," I begin, my voice low, "were once noble. My father stood against the Crown's brutal policies, against the way Isabella and Ferdinand consolidated power with blood and fire. For that, we lost everything. Titles, lands, honor. They stripped us down to nothing. Worse than any and all of that, my parents were executed. My sisters were taken. No trials, no graves. Just gone."

I watch her closely as I speak. The words are heavy, but they feel cathartic to say aloud.

"I was forced into exile, into the shadows," I continue. "Since then, I've served the resistance, those of us who refuse to bow quietly. We fight for those who cannot fight for themselves, for the forgotten and the broken."

Ava's eyes soften as I speak. She takes a breath before answering, her voice quiet but sincere. "I'm so sorry you lost your family, Luca. I can't imagine that kind of pain, or the void it leaves behind. If you ever want to talk about it, or simply not face it alone, you know where to find me."

She looks away for a moment, then back at me, tears brimming in her eyes. "There are deep wounds here, ones that have carved through this land for centuries… entire peoples, entire ways of life erased or forgotten. That sorrow is carried by those who remain."

I'm surprised by how deeply her words reach me, so simple, yet so true and kind. I fold the damp cloth, meeting her gaze. "Thank you for your words."

Lowering my voice, I press on. "There is a poison within our group, a betrayer among us. Signs are there: messages gone astray and those who vanish without cause. It threatens all we fight for."

I pause, wondering why I've shared this with her. Perhaps it is her disarming demeanor, or her lack of judgment that draws me.

"Luca, I will stand with you in this struggle. Whether it is guiding those who flee the city or aiding the resistance by whatever means you require."

I nod, feeling something shift between us, an unspoken alliance forming in the quiet kitchen as the night deepens.

After a moment, I break the silence. "Tomorrow night there's a celebration—the royal victory parade. I'm going."

Ava blinks, clearly surprised. "Why would you go to that?"

I meet her gaze steadily. "I'm going as a spy."

She nods. "I'll come with you."

* * *

THE NIGHT OF THE CELEBRATION COMES QUICKLY. TOLEDO'S STREETS are alive with lanterns and music, the city basking in the glow of a recent royal victory, although neither of us would call it that. What they celebrate as triumph, to us is an ending, not a beginning.

Ava and I move carefully through the crowd, our footsteps measured, our eyes alert. Tonight, we aren't mere spectators. We are spies blending into the revelry, searching for whispers of the threat that shadows us.

She wears a dress borrowed from one of the women on Abuela María's street, a soft, flowing garment of pale violet that catches the torchlight with every step. Her dark curls coil in wild waves, and in the glowing light, she looks both out of place and utterly captivating. To me, she belongs here, even as she stands apart.

The music swells and the crowd cheers, but beneath the celebration, I sense the undercurrent of tension. Ava leans close, her voice a low murmur. "They speak of the advisor—the one they want to strike."

I nod, muscles tightening. "We need to find out when and where."

Her eyes meet mine, and together, we slip deeper into the throng, weaving between dancers and torchbearers, hunting secrets hidden beneath the city's festive mask.

We move slowly, our eyes and ears alert, knowing full well that our purpose here isn't celebration but surveillance. We're not the only ones watching. I sense eyes scanning the crowd.

A murmur catches my attention near a cluster of merchants and city guards. The words are low, cautious, but carry a sharp edge that prickles my skin: "The advisor must fall before the moon wanes... no mistakes this time...."

"The Inquisition's grip tightens. His plans unravel if he lives...."

I exchange a glance with Ava. Her jaw tightens, and she leans in, her voice barely above a whisper. "The royal advisor, loyal to the Crown and the Inquisition. They want him dead."

I nod slowly, my thoughts flashing to the name whispered in darker corners of resistance circles: Miguel Pérez de Almazán. Not a warrior, not a priest, but something more dangerous, the one who drafts the decrees that destroy lives.

The gravity of it settles over the crowd's festive veil. There are whispers of treachery everywhere tonight, beneath the banners and the laughter. Someone in the monarchs' inner circle is marked for assassination.

As we move on, a band strikes up a lively tune, and the crowd swells to dance and cheer. Ava's eyes catch mine briefly, and there's something softer there. For a moment, the spy and the resistance fighter fade away, replaced by a woman and me, mesmerized by her.

We find a quieter street to skirt the festivities and make our way back toward Abuela María's house. The night air is cool, scented faintly with jasmine and burning wood from hearth fires. The torches behind us flicker like distant stars as we walk side by side, our footsteps echoing softly on the stones.

"I didn't expect to see this side of Toledo," Ava murmurs, brushing a curl from her face. "All this joy... after so much bloodshed. It's like they're celebrating a funeral and calling it a feast."

I glance at her, caught off guard by her honesty, and how precisely it mirrors my own thoughts. "They don't see it. Or maybe they choose not to. It's easier to cheer than to reckon with the truth."

She looks up, her blue eyes shining in the torchlight. "They don't care what this victory cost... what it will continue to cost. Families will continue to be torn apart. People will be hunted like animals."

A beat of silent sorrow passes between us.

"I wish I could believe this celebration meant peace," she says softly. "But all I see is the beginning of something darker. The Crown will not stop trying to erase your people, Luca."

I nod, my voice low. "I believe you are right."

There's a long silence as we walk, the city quieting around us.

Eventually, I ask, "Why did you come with me tonight?"

Her gaze drops to the ground, then back to me. "I want to help."

Ava's words are simple, yet, they stir something deep within me.

We stop beneath an ancient oak near the plaza, shadows wrapping around us like a secret. She steps closer, and I feel the warmth of her breath.

For a heartbeat, I want to reach out, to close the distance, but doubt claws at me–the uncertainty of who she truly is, and of what secrets she keeps locked away behind those hauntingly beautiful eyes.

I almost kiss her. The thought strikes so suddenly, it startles me, but I don't move. I just stand there, the space between us charged with something neither of us fully understands. There's too much I don't know about her, and that's what stops me.

I'm not sure if I'm falling in love with her, or walking straight into a trap.

7

# HOLY OFFICERS

## *AVA*

THE BREAKFAST on my plate has gone cold, barely touched. The morning sun streams through the small kitchen window as I sit in silence, my mind still back in the square last night, and in those shadowed alleys where secrets whispered louder than the drums.

I was brave last night and the day before. I offered to help Luca without hesitating. Promised to stand by him, to face whatever danger might come. At the time, it had felt easy, but only because I didn't believe any of it was real.

I had been telling myself this was a dream, a coma fantasy stitched together from half-remembered history books, Renaissance fairs, and period dramas. I thought I'd wake up at any moment, maybe in a hospital bed, Patrick at my side, my mom holding my hand.

When you think you're dreaming, it's easy to be fearless. It's easy to chase danger like it's part of a story you're playing out. It's easy, even fun, to offer yourself up like a hero when you believe you're untouchable.

But now, in the fragile light of morning, that illusion is crumbling. I'm not asleep. I'm not back home, and the longer I stay in this world, the more it feels like I may never leave it.

*What if I'm really stuck here?*

What if I never see my family again? Never hear Patrick laugh or text my sister or walk into Target like it's no big deal?

*What if I die here?*

"Ay, niña," Abuela Maria says gently, setting down a cup of tea in front of me. Her sharp eyes study my face. "Why are you so quiet this morning?"

I look up at her, startled, but say nothing. I don't know how to explain this weight sitting on my chest. I don't even know where to begin.

She doesn't press. She just sits beside me, her voice soft. "Sometimes the world is too large for our hearts to carry all at once. When that happens, we must share part of ourselves."

I look at her, the knot in my throat tightening.

She sips her tea, then continues, "You do good. You be brave. You choose kindness. That is all. The rest will fall into place."

I nod, not trusting my voice.

After breakfast, Abuela Maria tucks a bundle of neatly folded clothes into a basket, among them a dress I'd borrowed for the parade, and insists we walk them back. The breeze outside is warm, tugging at my sleeves and ruffling Abuela Maria's scarf as we make our way down the winding path. The village is just beginning to stir: a boy carrying firewood, two women laughing over a bucket of soapy linens, a dog asleep in the shade of a cart.

When we reach the cottage, Catalina greets us with a warm smile. She's around my age, maybe a little younger, and her arms are dusted with flour. "You didn't have to bring them back," she says, taking the basket with a grateful nod. "They looked better on you than they ever did on me."

I smile faintly. "Still, I wanted to thank you."

Before I can say more, a toddler appears at her skirt, clutching a wooden spoon and blinking up at me with enormous brown eyes. Another child follows, then a third, barefoot and giggling, hiding in a doorway.

"Come in, please," Catalina says, stepping aside. "I have a bit of cider cooling and my mother's dozing. It's quieter now than it will be all day."

Abuela Maria answers for both of us with a gracious nod, and soon we're inside the small, sunlit cottage. An elderly woman naps in a chair near the hearth. The children settle near a corner with wooden toys while Catalina pours us each a cup of cider.

"My husband will be returning for his noon meal soon," she says, handing me the warm mug. "The second he walks through the door, the children begin running and jumping again, but for just a moment, they may sit and play if we are lucky."

I nod slowly, trying to picture what my life would've looked like if I'd grown up here, if this had always been my world. How many children would I have? Would we have been able to stay together, or would we be torn apart the way Luca's family was?

She disappears for a moment, then returns with two more folded dresses. "You should keep these. I've outgrown them."

"Thank you," I say as I take them from her, stunned by her generosity. She probably only has a few dresses. These are soft and worn, the fabric patched but carefully mended. I run my fingers over the stitching, over seams that someone, probably Catalina herself, had fixed late at night after the children were asleep.

Something tightens in my chest. This isn't a dream. These people are real, and their lives are real. Their kindness, their struggle, their small, generous gestures–they're not figments of a fevered imagination.

Catalina's children laugh softly behind me. Abuela Maria thanks her again.

"Anything for you, Abuela," Catalina says warmly, brushing a strand of hair from her cheek as she balances her youngest on one hip. "You've helped me more times than I can count."

Just then, the front door creaks open and Catalina's husband steps inside, bringing a breeze of orange blossoms and wood smoke with him. He's tall and broad-shouldered, his tunic damp with sweat, his face lighting up as his children run to him squealing with excitement. He scoops one up into his arms with practiced ease and leans down to kiss Catalina on the cheek, their quiet affection unfolding right in front of me like something sacred.

I should look away, but I don't. My heart stirs as I watch him play with his children, hear Catalina's soft laughter, see the life they've built here. It's simple, but it's whole.

I wonder—*what would that life look like with Luca?*

I picture his arm around me. A child who looks like him. A home that smells like firewood and bread. A quiet, shared life in this strange world that doesn't feel so strange anymore.

Abuela Maria gently places a hand on my arm. "We should let them eat."

I nod, startled out of my thoughts. "Yes, of course."

We say our goodbyes, and Catalina squeezes my hand, saying, "You're welcome here anytime."

Abuela Maria and I walk quietly through the dusty streets, the basket now filled with dresses that smell like citrus soap. The air is thick with heat, but a breeze curls through the alleys, rustling linen from windows and stirring the hem of my borrowed skirt.

Back inside Maria's cottage, I set the basket down by the door and then, maybe because I'm tired, or maybe because I've started to care more than I meant to, I ask sheepishly, "Are you really everyone's Abuela?"

Abuela Maria chuckles, her laugh warm and low like a lullaby. "Not by blood, no. But I take care of people as though I am."

I smile, my heart tugging at the softness in her voice. "Luca calls you that."

She nods, turning back toward the kitchen to start a pot of stew. "He was just a boy when he came here. His parents were… gone. I made sure he ate, that he wore dry socks in the winter. He started calling me Abuela one day, and I never asked him to stop."

I don't know what to say to that. Only that it fits. Luca doesn't seem to belong to anyone, not really, and yet he belongs to everyone. He looks out for the people of these neighborhoods, plays games with the children, and carries water for the older men whose backs are too stiff to bend.

He's good in that effortless way. The kind of good that doesn't need to announce itself. I find myself wondering where he is now, what he's doing. If he's thinking about last night. If he almost kissed me, or if I just imagined that part.

It's my... what? Seventh? Ninth day here? I've lost track. Everything blurs together. The days bleed like watercolors.

I help Abuela Maria with a few evening chores, peeling root vegetables, sweeping ash from the fireplace, folding linens that smell like fruit and lavender. We eat a modest dinner of stew and flatbread in silence, and when I lie down that night, cocooned in a blanket on the bed by the window, I don't think of Patrick or my old apartment.

I think of Luca.

His voice. His handsome face. The way he hesitated just long enough to make me wonder what might have happened if we'd kissed.

* * *

SOMETIME DEEP IN THE NIGHT, I WAKE TO SHOUTING.

Not the usual drunk laughter or barked orders from guards. This is sharper and more urgent. A woman screams out in the street, and I sit up so fast the blanket falls to the floor.

Abuela Maria is already at the window. Her face is pale in the moonlight. I join her, peering through the slightly warped glass.

Down the street, torches bob in the darkness like fireflies. Hooded men in heavy robes stand outside a neighbor's house, the same one where a man waved to us yesterday, holding a baby on his lap. The same baby I smiled at.

Now, that man is on his knees in the dirt. Two men in gleaming armor hold him down while another reads from a scroll. His wife is screaming, clutching the baby to her chest. A young boy, maybe eight or nine, is shoved toward the wagon by a fourth man.

I cover my mouth. "What are they doing?"

Maria's voice is tight. "The Holy Officers of the Inquisition."

My stomach knots. The words hit like stones.

"They serve the king and queen directly," she whispers. "They don't answer to reason, or mercy."

The family is loaded into the cart. The man doesn't resist. He only keeps his eyes on his family as the torchlight recedes and the night grows quiet again.

Abuela Maria closes the shutters with a trembling hand, and I stand frozen for a long moment, caught somewhere between fear and disbelief. This isn't history class. It isn't a textbook chapter, a museum exhibit, or a lecture I listened to in college.

It's happening right here and now. And Luca—

My heart lurches.

*Where is he? What if he's next?*

8

# USE A DECOY

## *LUCA*

THE TAVERN IS LOUDER than usual tonight, packed shoulder to shoulder, the air thick with sweat and wine, but I can't shake the unease crawling down my spine. Something feels off. It started with whispers by the bread counter, then a barmaid hurrying past with wide eyes, muttering prayers under her breath.

Then I hear it.

"They're raiding houses in the northern quarter. Three families taken."

My blood runs cold. That's Abuela Maria's district.

I'm out the door before the man finishes speaking. The streets blur as I run, my boots pounding the road. *Please, let them be safe. Let them both be safe.*

I push past startled vendors, slip through alleys slick with oil and runoff. The breeze stings my eyes, but it's not the wind that makes my vision blur.

When I reach the edge of the quarter, I slow. I count the torches first. No flames in the streets. No soldiers. The homes are quiet and still. Abuela's door is shut, with no signs of force. I exhale deeply.

I knock twice. It opens, and there she is.

Ava's hair is wild around her face, her expression tired, yet alert,

49

like she hasn't slept. Abuela is behind her, whispering something I can't make out.

"You're all right," I say.

Ava steps aside to let me in. "We heard shouting. I saw—" Her voice breaks off. "Someone was taken."

I nod grimly. "Several were. The holy officers took three households. All for possessing forbidden documents."

Ava frowns. "What does that mean exactly? What did they contain that would count them as forbidden?"

"Texts in Arabic. Letters passed between families in Granada. Books that question doctrine, or speak of faiths other than Christianity. Anything not sanctioned by the Crown."

"And that's enough to—" Ava's voice trails off as understanding spreads across her face. "To drag children from their beds?"

"Yes." I meet her eyes. "It takes nothing more than paper and ink to be named a heretic."

She sways a little, and I reach out and steady her. "That's horrid."

"It is law." I keep my voice low, though the words burn in my throat. "And it is not just Moors and Jews they come for now. Even some Catholics can fall under suspicion if they help the wrong person. Anyone can be marked."

Ava crosses her arms. "That's... I mean, I knew life for many here was brutal, but—"

"But knowing and living it are not the same." I study her. "You are beginning to see."

Her jaw clenches. I can almost see the storm behind her eyes, the questions she wants to ask, the disbelief she's trying to swallow, and I have questions too. I have questions I've been pushing down since the day I found her mostly-drowned in the Tagus. Was she coming from the fortress that night? Or going to it? Do they know her there? Is knowing her, having her around, more dangerous than I've let myself admit?

Ava's eyes stay locked on mine, shining with something fierce, defiance or fear, I'm not sure. Perhaps both.

"What can be done?" she asks quietly. "To help them. The people they took."

I hesitate. The right answer is *nothing*. Not without risk. Not without drawing attention and fire toward ourselves.

"Please," she says. "Tell me."

I glance at Abuela Maria. She gives a subtle shake of her head, but says nothing. I know her warning. Don't pull the girl deeper.

"There's a meeting," I say. "Tonight. You can come with me."

* * *

WE WALK DOWN WINDING ALLEYS UNTIL WE REACH THE BACK OF THE wine merchant's cellar, a hidden door behind stacked casks of Tempranillo, invisible unless you know where to knock.

Inside, it smells of dust, wine, and smoke. One torch burns low. Men and women crouch around a low table: former scholars, Moorish poets, an old notary, a sailor who's run messages as far as Lisbon.

The meeting begins. Quiet voices trade news and rumors: who was taken, which scribe may be compromised, which guards can be bribed. There's talk of a boy hiding in the grain mill who needs to be moved before the next sweep.

We're deep in discussion when Tomás leans forward, his voice low and serious. "They're not kept in prisons like you might think. These families—men, women, children—they're held in guarded houses, warehouses, places where they hold them before ending them."

He glances around the room. "It's easier to move them quickly, in the night, before anyone knows they're gone. If we wait too long, they'll be scattered, sent away, or worse. We lose them completely."

Ava listens, silent at first, her eyes moving from face to face. Then she speaks, her voice cutting through the murmurs. "What if you used a decoy? Not someone to sneak out, but someone to send in."

Heads turn.

"To the place where they're held?" Tomás asks, skepticism in his tone.

"Yes," Ava says steadily. "Someone who can get through the gate. Someone who shows up with the right posture, the right story, bringing in food and supplies. It wouldn't have to make perfect sense. Just long enough to throw the guards off."

Inés narrows her eyes. "You think they'd fall for that?"

"They wouldn't have to fall for all of it. Just long enough to distract them. When they hesitate, when they look away even for a second, that's our window. That's when the real extraction happens."

There's a ripple of silence. Matius, ever the quietest among us, leans forward. "A decoy creates a bottleneck and slows the chain of command. If it's paired with a distraction outside, like a fire, loud noise, or both, they'll be split between responding to the chaos and confirming the orders."

Ava nods. "Exactly."

She sits back slightly, as if shying at the attention she's drawn. The others are murmuring, debating possibilities.

I watch her closely. There's a precision in her thinking, a cool, practiced way she lays out the moving parts of the plan. She sees the flaws before we name them. She suggests solutions faster than we can poke holes.

When the meeting finally breaks, one of the younger members of the group stops Ava. "You see things clearly," he says. "Don't lose that."

"Do you think it'll work?" she asks quietly.

He nods once. "Only one way to find out," he replies.

We step out of the wine cellar into a sky smeared with the faintest edge of morning. The stars are fading fast, but the moon still lingers, pale and watchful overhead. Ava's hood is pulled low, her arms folded across her chest against the chill, but there's a kind of fire in her stride now, quiet, focused, and tenacious. I say nothing as we slip through the narrow streets.

By the time we reach my door, the first birds are singing. I hesitate with the key in my hand. The right thing to do would be to escort her back to Abuela Maria's. It isn't proper for her to stay, but then I think of the soldiers prowling the streets, the names whispered in the cellar, the sharpness in Ava's voice when she asked what could be done.

Proper feels like a joke now. What use is decorum when the world is coming apart?

I unlock the door and push it open. "Please, come in."

She glances at me, and then nods, stepping inside without a word.

The room is quiet and dim, lit only by the coals left in the hearth. I stoke them gently, add a few slivers of kindling, and by the time the fire catches, the space feels warmer and safer.

"I'll make breakfast," I offer, already reaching for the skillet.

"You cook?" she says, one brow raised.

"Everyone learns when they live alone long enough," I answer, cracking a couple of eggs into the pan.

She watches me from the table, her arms wrapped around herself, not quite shivering, but close. I tear a hunk of yesterday's bread and set it to toast near the fire, then slide the eggs onto a plate, sprinkle a little salt, and hand it to her with a shrug. "It's not much, but it's warm."

"It's perfect. Thank you," she says.

She's halfway through her eggs when she says, "This is amazing, Luca. Thank you. You should let me cook for you sometime." As the fire burns low, she leans forward, chin resting on one hand, and asks, "What do you miss from home?"

I don't answer right away. It's not that I don't remember. It's that no one's asked me anything like that in a long time.

"Stories," I say finally. "My mother used to tell them while she sewed. Tales about foxes who tricked kings. Brave women who outwitted warlords. Magic that lived in rivers."

"Do you still remember them?"

"Some." I glance up at her.

I watch her as new daylight slips through the window, catching the fire's last glow in her eyes.

She rubs her eyes, voice barely above a whisper. "I feel like I haven't slept in weeks."

Without hesitation, I nod. "Then you should rest. My bed's free."

She pauses for a moment, then slowly moves toward the worn

mattress by the window. "Thank you, Luca," she says, sinking into my bed.

As I watch her drift off to sleep, I realize this remarkable woman is unlike anyone I've ever known, and I'm not ready to stop protecting her.

9

MY BABY JUST CARES FOR ME

*AVA*

THE LIGHT SLANTS differently when I wake, golden and lazy, spilling through the slants in the shutters. I sit up slowly in Luca's bed, the blanket still warm around me. From the other room comes the soft strumming of a lute. I swing my legs over the edge of the bed and step into the hall.

Luca sits in a worn wooden chair near the hearth, his fingers moving over the strings in perfect rhythm. He looks up as I appear. "I hope I didn't wake you."

"No," I say, rubbing the sleep from my eyes. "I needed to wake up anyway." I hesitate in the doorway, then nod toward the lute. "That sounds beautiful. Will you play another?"

A smile curves at the corner of his mouth, and he looks adorably surprised. "You want a song?" He teases.

"If you have one to spare," I flirt back.

He shifts, adjusts the instrument slightly, and begins to play again, this time a melodic tune that trills across the strings like birdsong. It's unfamiliar but comforting, like something meant to be remembered.

When the final notes fade, I say, "That was lovely. Thank you."

He bows his head bashfully. "My mother used to hum it when she rocked my baby sisters to sleep."

55

"I hope you'll teach it to me one day. Should we go check on Abuela Maria?" I ask.

He nods and stands, tucking the lute gently aside. "Yes. I'll walk you back."

We step out into the warm midday streets, the sun bright against the faded stone walls. I glance over at him. "How long have you been playing the lute?"

He shrugs with a grin. "Since I was a boy. My father taught me. Music's a kind of escape."

I nod. "It suits you. There's a gentleness in the way you play."

He chuckles. "Perhaps, but it's the only gentle thing about me."

"You're softer than you know," I say quietly.

We walk side by side through the winding streets until the familiar sight of Abuela Maria's house comes into view.

Inside, Maria sits by the window, tending to a pot of herbs. Her eyes brighten when she sees us.

Luca moves to her side. "How are you holding up?"

She smiles. "Better now that the two of you are here safe."

He touches her shoulder. "I'm so sorry for leaving again so soon, Abuela, but I should get back. There's still work to be done."

As he leaves, I watch the way he squares his shoulders against the quiet terror threaded through every corner of this city.

The sun has shifted to the west by the time I'm outside again, my sleeves rolled up, helping Abuela Maria string damp linen between ropes on wooden stakes. I twist and pin mindlessly, as my thoughts are on Luca.

Then a sharp, urgent knock sounds at the front door. Abuela stiffens beside me. I wipe my hands on my skirt, step through the back door, cross through the house, and open the front door.

A man I recognize from Luca's meetings stands on the stoop, his breath quick, his eyes moving nervously toward the street. "Good evening, Ava. My name is Tomás. I'm a friend of Luca. He needs you right away."

My pulse speeds up. "Is he hurt? Where is he? What does he need?"

"He isn't wounded. He's at the tavern," he says, already stepping back. "Everything is safe and secure. We just need your help. Please, come quickly."

I hesitate, but only for a second. I've seen Tomás before, at the meetings. I know he's one of Luca's most trusted men, and I've been to the tavern with Luca before. If the reason Luca needs me is urgent enough for Tomas to come all the way to the house, then it's urgent enough for me.

I turn over my shoulder. "I'll be back soon, Abuela Maria."

"Where are you—?"

"An errand for Luca," I say, and I'm already out the door.

Tomás keeps a rapid pace, and I follow. We move fast, weaving around a fish cart and past a gaggle of little boys chasing a chicken.

We slip behind a butcher's stall and descend a staircase into a tavern that smells like yeast and smoke.

Luca is already there, bent over a table lit by a single candle. "There's a shipment going into the holding compound at dusk," he says. "Crates of fruit. A forged order will get it through the gate."

A man beside him nods and slides a paper forward. The ink is still wet.

"There's a clerk inside who will be easy to fool," Luca goes on. "Matias will be able to lift the keys and open the holding cell before the distraction is complete."

My throat is dry. "What distraction?"

Luca meets my eyes. "You."

Someone presses a splintered crate into my arms. It smells like ripe figs.

"You'll walk in with Matias. All you have to do is draw the clerk's eye. Trip, drop something, recite poetry, it doesn't matter. Just long enough to shift attention while Matias grabs the keys and disappears. After you cause a distraction, we'll cause an even bigger one in the alley with noise and fire. That's when you run."

My hands tighten around the crate. "Why me?"

Luca looks at me steadily, his voice certain. "You're exotically beautiful," he says simply. "You don't look like anyone else here, not with those blue eyes. You're a distraction just standing still, but more than that," he continues, "you speak like no one else, stunning and strange. People will stop to listen, and if something goes wrong, I know you'll think of some clever way to get yourself and Matías out of trouble."

Luca is not just flattering me. He's putting real trust in my hands. Anxiety barrels through me at the thought of walking past the guards, risking capture, or worse, but beneath that fear is something heavier: the lives of those trapped in the compounds, counting on me. I've crossed a line. There's no turning back now.

I walk through the streets with my head down, the wooden crate pressed to my hip like a lifeline. My shawl itches at the back of my neck, and sweat trickles down my spine beneath the rough wool.

The man guiding me, Matías, doesn't speak. He carries a large box, a prop in our scheme, and his eyes scan everything. I follow just a step behind, trying not to look like a girl carrying lies through the middle of a city that eats people for smaller sins.

We reach the outskirts of the holding compound just as the sun begins to dip, painting the sandstone walls with a sickly orange glow. The outer courtyard is busier than I expected, with guards leaning against the walls, others laughing around a wine jug. We keep walking.

Matías tips his cap to the sentry, mutters something about the day's shipment. The man grunts and waves us toward the gate. For a moment, I think that's it—we've slipped through.

Then another voice cuts across the yard. "Wait."

A tall guard steps forward, too clean, too alert. He doesn't look bored like the others. He looks interested. "What's that?" he asks, nodding toward me.

My mouth goes dry. Matías tenses beside me, his eyes shooting toward the clerk standing near the guardhouse. While the guard's attention is on me, Matías slides a hand subtly to the clerk's belt.

His fingers close around a small key, and the oblivious clerk's gaze is still fixed on me. Matías slips the key into his own pocket.

"Delivery," I manage. "Fruit."

He frowns. "I didn't hear about an extra fruit crate coming through today."

Matías opens his mouth, probably ready to lie, but before he can, something inside me jolts into action. I take a breath, and my voice cuts through the air, clear, strong, and loud as a belt out the first song that comes to my mind, "My Baby Just Cares for Me."

The words are strange and foreign here. Not a chant or a hymn from Castilla. It's soulful jazz, and what's more, I'm singing it in English, bold and out of place in this dusty old courtyard.

The guards freeze. One narrows his eyes, confused. Another crosses his arms, muttering under his breath, but he doesn't try to stop me. A third shifts uneasily, caught between suspicion and curiosity.

I sway to the rhythm seductively, and keep singing, easier now, louder.

Beside me, I feel Matías move—no sudden motion, just a slow shift and step, quiet as a shadow slipping away. He slides toward the back wall, melts into the darkness, and disappears.

I don't look. I reach the next lines, my voice rising and hips rolling in an attempt to entrance the guards.

They're listening. The melody hangs between us, haunting me like an answered prayer from another lifetime.

Then I hear a thunderous crack, so loud it feels like the earth itself flinches. The night outside the compound flares bright, orange, then white, before smoke begins to curl over the walls.

Shouts rise in confusion, and boots scramble as the guards jolt into motion. Most of them take off at a sprint. In the chaos, no one notices me slip back into the shadows. The darkness swallows me l before they even realize I'm gone.

I don't stop running until I slip into the narrow shadowed alley where Luca waits, his silhouette barely visible in the dark.

He catches my arm, holding me as I breathlessly struggle to stay upright. "You did it," he says, eyes filled with awe. "You saved them. Matías and the others will be waiting, hiding in the barns behind the market."

Without hesitation, we race through the backstreets until the barn comes into view. Inside, a dim back room behind the goat stalls is filled with hushed voices and restless movement. One by one, the families who slipped past the unlocked holding cell doors are here, and alive with hope.

Matías steps forward, his eyes shining as he spots me. "You were their angel," he says quietly. "Without you, none of this would've happened."

Whispers of gratitude and relief ripple through the gathered crowd as I walk through. I feel Luca's hand find mine, firm and grounding. They all look at me like I carried the impossible on my shoulders, but all I did was sing.

Beyond these walls, more allies wait: safe houses ready, secret paths mapped, hands willing to guide each of these souls far from the Crown's grasp.

Tonight, we've done more than free prisoners. We've sparked a flame no darkness can easily snuff out. I know now that I'm a fugitive. There's no way they won't tie me to this prison break, but I don't care. This isn't a dream. It's real.

All I want is to help the ones being hunted in Toledo.

# 10

# I WILL RETURN

## *LUCA*

THE BARN WALLS sweat in the torchlight as we crowd inside, breathless and shaking, but alive. The chains are broken. The doors were forced open. Our people, dragged from homes and workshops in the dead of night, are free.

Ava stands beside me, her cheeks flushed, with curls clinging to her forehead. Her eyes scan the room, counting survivors before I do.

Matías bolts the door behind us. "No one followed," he says.

"You did well," I tell him, my voice low. "You both did. Quick thinking."

"I thought we were going to die," he says with a shaky laugh. "But then it worked."

I move through the huddled group, checking injuries. A boy holds a hand to his ribs. An older woman won't stop coughing. I kneel beside her, pressing a cold cloth to her forehead. Ava is already crouched beside another man, examining a gash on his arm. They weren't harmed in the explosion. That was just Luis and Martin shooting off fireworks in the alley. Sadly, the reason that these people are injured is because the guards roughed them up.

Ava looks up at me. "What now?"

"We split them into three small groups, taking different routes.

One goes south across the river. One travels by cart with forged permits. The third will take the path north through the olive groves."

"Will they be safe?"

I hesitate. "They'll be safer than they would've, had they stayed locked away. I stand, raising my voice a little. "We move at once. They'll sweep the city when they find the cells empty."

Matías comes up behind me, his voice clipped. "It's like they knew someone was coming, but they didn't know what it was. The west road near the alley where the fire was set was too heavily guarded."

I glance at him, then at Ava. Her brow furrows.

"Bad luck," I offer. "Or someone speaking out of turn."

Ava doesn't flinch. "Then we keep the next steps quieter."

She's sharp, and she doesn't scare easily. As I watch her move through the freed prisoners, touching shoulders, helping dress wounds, I realize I'm falling for this woman. Not just for her courage, but for the strength she carries in moments like this. Her presence seems to calm everyone around her, even as the tension tightens.

By the time the worst wounds are wrapped and the plans whispered to each group, it's dark. The barn empties in quiet waves, boots muffled against dirt floors, nerves on edge.

I walk Ava back myself, telling Matías I need to check on Abuela María, but honestly, I don't want to send Ava home alone. She is most likely being hunted now too.

The streets are quiet, shadows pooling deep in the narrow alleys. Every distant footstep or creak of a shutter sends a jolt through the stillness, reminding us how close danger always is.

"I still don't know how we pulled it off," Ava says softly. "I keep expecting someone to shout after us."

I glance around. "Don't say that out loud again."

She nods, placing a finger over her lips, a silent promise. I reach out and curl my hand around hers, pulling it gently away, but not letting go. Our fingers stay linked, warm and comforting in the dark.

We reach Abuela María's door just as she's opening it. Her night shawl is still draped over her shoulders. She must've been watching for us through the window.

"Ay, niña," she murmurs, pulling Ava into her arms. "Gracias a Dios."

Then she looks past Ava, at me. Her eyes scan my face, checking for wounds, for tiredness I won't admit. "You're staying," she says, as if she already decided for me.

"I thought I might. Just for a few hours. In case—"

She nods enthusiastically. "I'll make you some food."

I don't argue. She wants me here where she can keep an eye on me, and it soothes her.

When Ava brushes past on her way inside, our shoulders touch, and the warmth lingers longer than it should. That's reason enough to stay.

I settle into an old chair as Abuela María lights the stove, and Ava slips into the back room, perhaps to change, or cry, or just catch her breath.

María doesn't ask for details. She just moves through the kitchen like she always does, pulling things from jars, cracking eggs into a bowl with practiced movements. The smells are familiar, garlic, onions, and oil hitting a hot pan.

"You need to eat," she says, glancing at me like she can see right through the fatigue stitched into my bones.

I don't argue. I just lean back against the cushion. The chair sags beneath me, and the warmth from the fire creeps over my bones. A faint clatter of forks, oil sizzling, and somewhere behind me, Ava's soft footsteps.

I close my eyes, just for a second, and that second stretches. I don't feel myself falling asleep, but when I open my eyes again, the room is flooded with morning light.

The skillet is cold on the stove. A plate sits on the side table beside me, covered with a cloth, untouched, and there's a blanket over my shoulders, one I don't remember pulling up.

I turn my head to see Abuela María seated across the room, darning a sock. She glances up, gives me a nod. No words, just a quiet acknowledgment.

I sit up slowly, brushing the blanket back. My joints ache less than they did. My mind feels clearer as I rise from the chair. María watches me with tired eyes, offering a small nod when I speak of moving Ava out of the city.

Toledo is undoubtedly already humming with whispers about the woman with blue eyes who turned the prison upside down. Ava is marked now, and staying here is too dangerous.

I find her sitting by the kitchen window, her fingers tracing the carved wood frame.

"We have to get you out of the city," I say gently. "Somewhere quiet and safe."

Her gaze meets mine. "I'm ready."

Before we slip away, Abuela Maria pulls Ava aside. I watch as she hands her something wrapped in cloth. Ava unwraps it, revealing her fine gown, mended and clean. Ava's eyes well up with tears, the gratitude clear as she clutches the gown to her chest. She places it in her satchel with some other clothing.

I help her gather what little supplies we have, careful not to draw attention as we slip through the sleeping streets. The city walls loom behind us, pale in the starlight, but ahead lies open country, wild, and waiting.

Not far beyond the olive groves, I lead her down a hidden trail, one only a few in the resistance know. Tucked behind an abandoned shepherd's hut is a grove where we've kept a few horses in reserve, for moments just like this. I ready two quickly, their breath rising in soft clouds, their ears twitching in the quiet.

We ride hard, following old roads and deer paths over the hills. The wind cuts sharply across the fields, but Ava doesn't complain. She holds fast behind me, Toledo fading in the distance.

By the time we reach the edge of the village, the sky has paled. Smoke curls lazily from a chimney. A dog barks nearby, but otherwise, the world is quiet. It is a safe place for Ava, for now.

We dismount beside a weathered stone wall. She steps away, her arms folded against the chill, and I can feel the question trembling in her posture before she even speaks.

"What happens now?" Her voice is soft, roughened by wind and fear.

I don't answer right away. I watch her, the way her hair clings to her cheek, the way her eyes hold mine like she's searching for something solid to hold on to.

"You stay," I say finally. "Lie low. Keep your head down. You'll be safe here."

"When will I see you again?"

I step closer, close enough to feel the heat of her skin, the tension in her muscles. I lift my hand slowly, brushing a strand of hair behind her ear, letting my fingers linger just for a second.

"No matter what happens," I whisper, "no matter how long it takes, how far I have to go, I will return to you."

Her eyes shimmer in the faint light, full of everything she's not saying.

The farmhouse crouches low at the edge of the valley, half-swallowed by trees and dusk. A soft yellow light flickers behind the shutters.

We walk the last stretch together, pebbles crunching underfoot. I didn't send word ahead. There was no time, no safe route, and still, I'm betting everything on their kindness.

I knock. There's a pause, then the sound of movement inside. A latch lifts, and the door creaks open.

My friend Diego stands there in shirtsleeves, a little flour on his hands, his eyes narrowing in confusion when he sees me and filling with curiosity when he sees Ava beside me.

"Luca?" he asks cautiously.

"We need a place," I say quickly. "Just for a little while. She's not safe in the city."

He glances over his shoulder, then steps aside without another word.

His wife, Raquel, appears from the kitchen, drying her hands on her apron, her gaze moving from my face to Ava's. There's no alarm in her eyes, only concern. Behind her, a young girl peers around the corner.

"Come in," the woman says softly.

We step inside, and the warmth of the house spills out as we cross the threshold.

"This is Ava," I tell them. "She needs a place to lie low for a while."

"Welcome, Ava," Raquel says, reaching to squeeze Ava's shoulder gently. "We'll take care of you here."

"I don't know how to thank you," Ava replies.

I place her satchel just inside the door, and she turns to me. Her eyes search mine, full of questions I can't answer yet.

"I'll come back," I say. "As soon as I can without being followed."

She nods once, and I touch her hand. If we speak, I won't leave. So, I turn before the silence can crack open between us and walk back to the horses. The door closes behind me.

The road is bathed in moonlight, but everything ahead feels darker than what I've left behind. I don't know what danger I'm riding into, only that it's colder and quieter without her.

I keep moving, but the ache for Ava stays with me.

11

# NOT ALONE

## *AVA*

THE HOUSE SMELLS of rosemary and wood smoke. I sit near the hearth, my hands folded in my lap, as Raquel introduces each of her young children. Two little girls with thick dark braids cling to her skirt, and a younger boy, barefoot and sleepy-eyed, leans against Diego's leg. They're warm, safe, and so far from everything I just left behind in Toledo.

I barely speak. The song I sang still echoes in my mind, the one that bought the others their chance to run. Now, that song feels like a beacon, drawing eyes and danger straight to me.

I'm scared. Not just of what's out there, but of what will happen if they find me here. In Toledo, the price for what I did is death.

I force myself to smile at the carved wooden toy pressed into my palm. I'm not dreaming. I'm really in Castile during the Spanish Inquisition, and I'm in danger.

Later, as we sit around the table, I ask, "What's the name of this village?"

"Cobisa," Diego says. "It's small, with just a few homes, a chapel, olive groves. Far enough from Toledo to be quiet and safe, but close enough that it doesn't take long on horseback to fetch something or someone from the city."

Raquel sets a bowl of grapes in front of me and gives my shoulder a light squeeze, and I'm grateful that she doesn't ask questions.

Two young men I recognize from the meetings step in through the back door. Diego rises, smiling.

"These are our oldest sons," he says proudly. "Luis and Martin. Sons, this is a friend of Luca's. Her name is Ava."

They both nod, their expressions curious. Martin looks like Raquel, and Luis has Diego's eyes. Neither seems surprised to find me here.

"How do you know Luca?" I ask softly.

"We grew up together," Diego explains. "Our families farmed the land in this part of the country. His father's plot was taken years ago, by politics, religion, and the Crown. We were luckier."

Raquel glances at him, then back at me. "Diego's grandfather converted," she says simply. "Publicly. And Diego's cousin married into a noble family who still holds favor at court. That helped when they started taking people's property."

*Moriscos.* That's what they'll be called one day. In this generation the word hasn't been spoken yet, but I know enough history to recognize what they're risking just by letting me in the door, and I am astonished by their courage and kindness.

I turn toward Luis and Martin. "And the two of you are involved in the rebellion as well?"

Luis sits beside the fire, stretching out his legs. "We are. We're the ones who set off the explosions, and we heard about what you did," he says.

Martin adds, "People are still marveling over what you pulled off."

I glance at Luis and Martin, feeling a swell of gratitude and hope. "It's good," I say, "that all of you are working together, finding ways to fight back, even when the odds feel impossible."

Luis nods. "We have to for our families, and for the future of our culture. We are just normal people, trying to live peacefully."

Martin adds, "Our legacy will be that when the Crown tried to use the cross to fuel their filthy greed, we stood our ground. There are more similarities than differences when it comes to the vast religious beliefs and core values of our nation, and yet, the king and queen who rule today, want to silence and divide what could be celebrated and unified."

"Well said," I murmur, amazed that someone as young as Martin could speak with such eloquence, capturing the essence of this moment in time so beautifully, though tragic.

Before I can say more, Raquel's voice cuts gently through the room. "Ava, I'm sure you're tired. Would you like to rest?"

She stands and takes my hand, leading me toward a narrow stairway. "There's a loft upstairs. It's simple, but it's yours for as long as you need." Her kindness settles over me as I follow her into the silent shelter of the room above.

There's a small cot and a low chest pressed against the wall. Raquel sets a candle on the chest, its light pooling weakly against the worn wooden walls. As soon as the door closes behind her, I lie down in my clothes, and sleep swallows me whole.

* * *

I wake only once to the sound of rain tapping against the roof, long enough to drink water someone has left by the cot. My body feels like it's made of stone. When I blink again, the candle is gone, and it's dark. Still, I drift back into sleep without fighting it.

I don't know how long I've been asleep, but when my eyes open next, the sky beyond the small window is deep indigo. The house is silent, the fire downstairs burning low. I can smell the faintest curl of smoke, but there are no voices, no footsteps. Just the hush of a family sleeping, and the rapid beat of my own thoughts.

That's when it hits me. An image from a book I once read, or maybe a lecture–it's difficult to say now–about ancient Toledan architecture and ritual spaces hidden beneath cities. A bathhouse. Mikveh, maybe, or something older. I remember walking near the entrance of one with Luca, near an old fountain in the Jewish quarter. Luca didn't point it out to me, and I wonder if he even knows it's there.

I ease myself out of bed, shivering as my bare feet touch the cold wooden floor. Without a sound, so as not to wake anyone, guided only by moonlight, I rummage through the worn chest. I find a small stack of rough parchment, take one sheet, along with a stub of charcoal wrapped in cloth, and settle onto the floor, ready to write.

*In the Jewish quarter, east of the old fountain, lies a buried and forgotten bathhouse. Its tunnels run deep. Use it at twilight.*

I fold it carefully and slip it beneath my pillow.

At breakfast, I find Luis and Martin at the table, hunched over bowls of fresh fruit. Raquel moves behind them, refilling teacups and slicing bread.

"I need to give you something," I say, stepping closer and holding out the folded note. "It's for Luca, but don't tell him who it's from."

Martin glances up, his brow lifting.

Luis takes the letter and tucks it into his tunic without a word. "You trust us that much?" he asks.

I nod once. "You're helping save my life. I'm trying to return the favor."

Luis and Martin exchange a glance, then Luis nods. "We will as soon as we finish eating."

Martin adds, "He won't hear your name from us."

True to their word, they rise as soon as the last bite is gone, slipping out the door with purpose, the letter tucked safely against Luis's chest.

* * *

Raquel presses her youngest to her shoulder, gently patting his back, and I reach for a cloth to wipe his chin. The kitchen is filled with the smell of simmering garlic, the hum of a household winding down. The sun is in the west when Luis and Martin step in through the back door, dust clinging to their boots and sleeves.

"We're heading to the old bathhouse," Martin says, his voice low. "Figured you might want to come with us."

I set the cloth down, my heartbeat accelerating. "Yes, of course."

I follow them outside, where three saddled horses await. We follow a narrow path through a grove of cypress and fig trees, the road winding toward the remains of the old water mill outside of Toledo.

When we reach the ancient bathhouse, I know it instantly. Beneath the collapsed stone wall is the narrow opening, half-blocked by rubble but still passable. Martin dismounts first and leads the way, pushing aside the loose rock. We move quickly, ducking into the cool mouth of the tunnel, our boots scraping over the packed earth.

Inside, it looks exactly as I pictured: low-arched, timeworn, echoing faintly with the breath of the past. It smells and tastes of chalky minerals.

A lantern glows in the distance, and then I hear his voice.

"Luis? Martin?"

Luca steps out of the shadows, a satchel over his shoulder, his cloak pushed back. His hair's tousled, and there's dirt smudged across his temple. He still looks handsome even when he looks like he hasn't slept, and when his eyes land on me, he stops cold.

"Ava?"

I freeze too.

His expression is of shock, confusion, and then something I can only describe as raw, unfiltered relief.

"You're—" He begins, then he laughs, stepping closer. "You're here. But why? How?"

"These fine men invited me," I say, trying to keep my voice calm and steady. "They said they were involved in your work, that you needed help. I… just came with them."

Luis and Martin exchange a quick glance and nod, then slip into the adjoining chamber where the others wait. Their footsteps fade into the shadows, leaving the cool stillness around Luca and me.

He reaches me in two long strides. I think he's going to scold me, tell me it was too risky, or ask why I didn't stay hidden, but instead, he pulls me into an embrace, and the feel of his biceps and chest against my body is enough to make me melt.

"I got an anonymous note about this place," he murmurs. "I

checked it out first, and it's completely abandoned. It's perfect, but I didn't think I'd see you here—" He breaks off, his eyes scanning my face. "I missed you," he says, so softly I almost don't catch it.

"I missed you too."

We stand just inside the dim tunnel, the faint lantern light glowing.

"I didn't expect you to be here," he murmurs, his voice gravelly.

"Neither did I," I whisper.

Then his lips brush against mine. His hand lifts, resting gently on my waist. The kiss deepens, like a slow building fire. His kiss is firm, his lips soft, and in the way he holds me, I feel the intensity of his passion.

I don't know what waits for me beyond these walls. Whether the guards are closing in, or if my name's already been whispered through the streets, but right now, I'm here with Luca, and somehow, in the strength of his arms, I feel safe.

Not because the danger's gone, but because I'm not facing it alone.

# 12

# TOLEDO NEVER SLEEPS

## *LUCA*

I HAVE KNOWN the weight of war, the taste of blood, the ache of loss. I have carried it all, and yet nothing could have prepared me for her.

Ava—clever, loyal, brave as any warrior, with beauty that strikes like lightning, and yet, somehow, she is also the best kisser a man could ever hope to find. It defies sense. If I fall tomorrow, if I am laid in the earth with the rest of the dead, I will go to my grave with the memory of that kiss on my lips, and count myself a fortunate man for it.

"We should probably—" She speaks breathlessly.

"You're right," I say. "The others are waiting."

We leave the mouth of the bathhouse and follow the narrow passage until we reach the iron door to the main chamber. I stop with my hand on the latch.

"Your presence is a blessing," I say. "We'll speak after the meeting."

Ava smiles, nods, and we step inside. The old bathhouse is cold and cavernous, the echo of dripping water accenting every movement. A few torches flicker along the stone walls. Roots and vines have split some of the tiles, and a few of the benches are cracked, but it's safe, hidden, and most importantly, ours.

Ramon lifts a brow. "About time."

Luis chuckles. "Thought you got lost in the dark."

Martin leans back on a crumbled column. "If this place is as untouched as it looks, we might've just struck gold."

I raise a hand, and the room settles. "This place," I say, "is more than shelter."

Their attention locks in.

"It's a fortress no one remembers. Forgotten by the castle, ignored by the patrols. That's exactly what we need. Starting tonight, this becomes our hideout, and our base."

Ramon whistles low. "Could use a few hammocks, but I'm in."

"There's more," I continue. "We've only explored the main halls. There are tunnels branching deeper. Some might connect to the aqueducts, or to the edge of the city. Once we've mapped it, this won't just be a hiding place. It'll be a passage out."

The group exchanges looks. Their excitement is real and alive.

"But I need to speak plainly," I add, letting my voice drop. "We've got a leak."

That silences them.

"Too many near misses. Too many exact locations known. We don't have proof yet, but someone's been passing information to the guards. I don't care if it's fear or money. If it's someone in this room, or connected to someone here, we will find out."

I glance at Matius and Tomas standing behind me, their faces set hard as stone.

"They're here to deal with whoever's responsible," I say. "And if we find the traitor, we won't hesitate. No warnings. No mercy. No matter who it is. They've risked all our lives."

Martin speaks up. "If someone's selling us out, we'll bury them."

Ramon nods. "If anyone is working against us, we'll bury their name with them."

"Good," I say. "Now, we've got work to do. We've confirmed that at least six of our people were picked up by the guards last night and are being held without trial."

Murmurs ripple. A few fists clench.

"They're being held in a temporary compound north of the

barracks. At dawn, four of you are moving. Quiet, fast, and even brutal if you have to be. You'll get them out and take them beyond the city walls. This is the beginning of a new phase in our plan," I say. "This bathhouse, this mission. We aren't just surviving anymore. We're building something. I'll pick five of you, and you'll get with Tomas for a detailed plan of attack."

The men nod, the pressure of the task settling over them. I catch Ava's gaze. She'd probably volunteer to join the rescue mission if I'd let her, but I'm not even going. I have a different task, one I have to handle alone.

When the council draws to a close, the men gather their gear and file toward the tunnels, their voices low and certain.

Ava stands near one of the stone pillars, her cloak gathered around her, but her expression softens when her eyes meet mine. It hits me again how much I wasn't expecting to see her tonight, and how much I don't want her to leave now.

I take a step closer. The torchlight glows against the carved walls, casting her in warm shadows. "I wish you didn't have to go."

"I wish I didn't either. Or that you could come with me."

I nod, and without another word, I step closer and pull her into my arms. My hands settle at her waist as hers come up to my chest, and I kiss her again, slower this time.

When the kiss breaks, I keep my eyes locked on the curve of her breasts, the way her body moves beneath the cloak. I'm drawn in, every part of me aching to hold on.

"I'll see you soon?" she asks.

"You'd better," I say. Words fall short of what I want to say, but I hope they're enough.

I lead her up the slick stone steps to the mouth of the bathhouse. Luis stands by the entrance, his eyes sharp and alert, as he says, "We'll get her home safely."

Martin adds, "No mistakes tonight."

We leave in opposite directions, her with Luis and Martin, me back toward the city.

Her kiss still smolders on my lips, and every part of me wants to hold on to her, but the city needs me. I can't lose focus, not now, not when everything depends on what comes next.

* * *

TOLEDO NEVER SLEEPS, AND NEITHER DO THE SECRETS IT HIDES. Tonight, I'm chasing one of those secrets: a rat eating away at us from inside.

I stole a guard's uniform a while back. I didn't think much of it then, just figured I'd need it, eventually. I never expected I'd end up wearing it to hunt a mole leaking plans, blending in as I watch and wait.

I move fast through narrow alleys, every step silent on the wet cobblestones. My hands twitch, itching for the weight of my sword, but this is a different kind of fight. The rebellion's out there, bleeding and hunted, and I need every scrap of their enemies' mysteries if I want to keep us alive.

The tavern door groans as I push inside, and a wall of heat and stench crashes over me—sweat, smoke, and stale ale. The room is packed tight, bodies pressed close, their voices rough and sharp beneath the low flicker of lantern light. I order a tankard of watered-down ale, more for the act than the taste.

I don't drink much, just enough to blend in. I scan faces, catching flashes of steel, calloused hands, hardened expressions. They're drunk, and names will slip out here.

The guards talk patrols, missing boots, grumbling about low pay. Then, like a blade sliding free from its sheath, I catch it.

"...heard it from the captain himself," a deep voice mutters, low and urgent. "We got a man on the inside. Been feeding us their every move—the rebels' plans, their shifts."

My fingers curl tight around my mug. That's the rat I've been hunting.

Another guard scoffs. "They should've known one of their own would rat them out. Not a one of them loyal."

I keep still, listening.

The first voice, louder this time. "But the last raid? We knew exactly where they were. Wasn't even fun to hunt 'em."

I swallow the bitter ale, tasting ash. The rage inside me burns hot. I listen more carefully, hoping for a name, a clue, anything.

The talk drifts back to griping about food and schedules. I down the last of my drink and rise.

Then the mouthiest guard's cloak catches my eye. A piece of parchment pokes from his pocket.

As the guards laugh and shout, I edge near, my hand slipping like a shadow. Quick as a blink, I snatch the parchment and tuck it into my own pocket.

The tavern roars behind me as I slip through the back exit, the stolen paper tucked deep in my pocket. I keep my head down and my pace steady, disappearing into the streets of Toledo.

I'm still moving when I pull the paper from my pocket, and one glance tells me enough. It's a code, and not a simple cipher either—layered, deliberate, and meant to hide something important. I don't know what it says, but I know who can figure it out.

The stable's not far. I find my horse tied loosely, a bay mare with eyes sharp as a hawk's. I swing up fast, no time to lose. The streets blur past, Toledo asleep while I ride hard through the dark, headed straight for her.

I push the mare hard, hooves pounding the earth as we break free from the city's grasp, racing toward the countryside, toward Ava.

Dawn's first pale fingers brush the sky by the time I reach the small house where Ava's staying. It's a simple place, Diego and Raquel's home, a refuge far from the city's chaos.

I dismount, tie the mare to the post, and head up the steps, rapping my knuckles sharply on the weathered wood.

Diego opens the door with a grin and pulls me into a quick, familiar hug. "You're up early, or out late more likely. Do you ever sleep? And why are you dressed as a guard?" he asks, stepping aside to let me in. The smell of eggs and bread hits me as I step into the warmth.

Their little ones are already tearing through the kitchen, shrieking and laughing, and I reach out to ruffle the hair on one of their heads as they bolt past. The house is full of life, messy, warm, and familiar.

Raquel glances over her shoulder from the hearth, a wooden spoon in one hand. "Look who's finally come around," she teases.

Ava looks up from the counter, her hands still mid-motion over a loaf of bread. She drops what she's doing, steps forward, and throws her arms around me, holding on tight.

"Luca," she says. "What are you doing here?"

I hold her for a beat, the noise of the kitchen fading away. When she finally pulls back, her cheeks are flushed, but her eyes are bright.

I pull the folded parchment from inside my cloak and pass it to her. "Found this at the guards' tavern. It looks like a code. I thought you might take a look."

"Ah, so that's why you're dressed as a guard," Diego says. "Well, if you're going to refuse to sleep, will you at least eat?" he asks, passing me a plate.

Ava carries the parchment to the table and spreads it out carefully, smoothing the creases like she's unwrapping something important. "Where'd you get this?" she asks, already scanning the marks.

"I took it from a guard," I say. "Can you figure it out?"

I watch her work, the tilt of her head, tracing lines and symbols, the way her brow furrows in concentration. The more I watch, the more I realize how much this woman knows, and how much I need her.

Hours slip away while Ava deciphers the code, the sun climbing high and painting the room with golden light. Diego and Raquel bring food and drink, but neither of us remembers to eat.

Luis and Martin stop by to grab a quick meal after their rescue mission at dawn. They bring word that the mission was successful, eat fast, and once they're done, I send them back out on another errand in Toledo.

Piece by piece, Ava cracks the code. Every discovery feels like a victory, but it's her mind I admire most.

"You make this look easy," I say, my voice rough.

"It's just a matter of knowing where to look."

I lean closer, watching her sapphire eyes sparkle.

* * *

That night, the fire burns low, and the candlelight casts soft shadows on the rough wooden table. Diego, Raquel, and their children are asleep in the next room.

Ava leans over the parchment, her eyes sharp, her brow furrowed as she cracks the last symbols of the code. I want to tell her how much that shakes me. How much I admire her, but the words stick in my throat.

Instead, she yawns, tired but stubborn. I reach out without thinking. My fingers move on their own, gently tucking the stray hair behind her ear. Our eyes meet, and I lean in, my heart pounding.

Then the door bursts open. Luis and Martin stumble in, their faces pale and their eyes wild with panic.

"The prison compound," Martin gasps, breath ragged. "It's burning, and many of ours are still inside."

The moment is gone.

I push back from the table, muscles tight and ready to move.

Ava's eyes flash with fire, the same spark I saw all day, only now it's sharpened by urgency.

I pull on my cloak and head for the door. I won't waste another minute while the Crown sharpens its blade, not when someone among us might've helped them wield it.

13

—————

# I'D CHOOSE LUCA

### *AVA*

MARTIN'S WORDS hit like a slap, and the romantic moment Luca and I almost had vanishes. More importantly, I never got to tell him I cracked the code.

After hours of work, it finally broke open beneath my fingertips. I figured out the message mere seconds before Luca almost kissed me. Before Luis and Martin burst in, and now the compound's burning, and Luca's already heading for the door.

I grab his arm. "Wait—I figured it out," I say, my voice filled with urgency. "The code. I broke it. There's a message."

He stops, his eyes locking on mine, but before either of us can speak again, footsteps rush down the hall. Diego appears first, blade in hand, his eyes moving over the room, taking in Luis and Martin, still catching their breath. Raquel follows just behind, her shawl pulled tight, alarm written all over her face. "What's going on?" she asks, already bracing for the answer.

"The prison compound's burning," Luca says. "We have to go."

Turning to me, he continues, "Wait, did you say that you figured it out?"

"Yes. It's signed RF," I explain. "The rat is whoever RF is. They have been helping the guards. The message gives the exact time to

81

burn the compound, and they were foolish enough to sign their initials, albeit encoded. If we don't stop them, they'll tell the guards about the bathhouse."

Luca tenses beside me, his jaw tight. "RF is Ramon. I thought he'd been acting a little overzealous lately. He was trying to cover his treacherous tracks. We don't have a second to waste. We're heading back to Toledo. Now."

We move fast, grabbing saddles and strapping on gear. Luca, Luis, Martin, and I mount, the night air biting as we gallop through the dark. The fire will be waiting, and so will Ramón. We're coming for both.

The glow of the fire grows brighter as we near the compound, a raging, hellish beacon against the night sky. The acrid smell of smoke stings my nostrils even before we reach the walls.

At the edge, chaos reigns. Shouts crack through the night—men scrambling, hauling prisoners from the flames. Guards move in tight patrols, their eyes sharp, weapons ready. Tomas and Matius are already here, trying to slip past the guards, dragging people to safety. Their faces are set, grim and unyielding.

I stay close to the shadows, my heart pounding, not brave enough to dive into the fray. The risk of being seen is too great.

Luca moves like a ghost among the others, quick and sure, his eyes scanning the scene. When he pulls Tomas and Matius aside for a quick, low conversation, I slip close enough to catch every word.

"Ramon's the rat," Luca says, his voice cold and sharp. "He's been feeding the guards everything. Tomas, Matius—find him. End him quietly."

I hold my breath, the weight of those words settling heavy in my chest. There's a strange, terrible thrill in it, sharp and electric, and beneath that is fear. The knowledge that I'm caught in a world that could destroy me.

Yet even with all the danger and risk, I find myself drawn to Luca, and the way he carries the burdens of so many with fierce determination. A part of me aches to return to my own time, to safety, but another part is tethered here, tangled up in him.

Later, after we've hidden the injured, and the smoke starts to thin, Luca and I settle in the bathhouse. My hands shake as I brush soot from my cheeks.

"They want us to lash out," I say softly. "So they can crush us in daylight… not shadows."

Luca nods. "We must gather everyone. We must guard the bathhouse and come up with a new plan."

We all return to the bathhouse, the terror of the night pressing in on us. Some, Luca among them, haven't slept in days. Exhaustion drapes over the group, but none of us dare lower our guard. We take turns resting, cycling between sleep and watch.

Luca stands near the entrance, his arms crossed, tension bleeding from every inch of him.

A hidden door groans open, and Luca turns fast, his hand already on the hilt at his hip, but it's Tomas who steps in, with Matius close behind. Both are flushed from the heat, their clothes dusty from the tunnels.

"It's done," Tomas says without ceremony. "Ramon's not going to talk."

Luca doesn't move. "Dead?"

Tomas nods once. "Buried deep. Where no one will find him."

"And before that?" Luca asks. "Did he talk to anyone? Pass a note? Look at someone too long?"

Matius steps forward, his jaw tight. "We watched the street. No one followed. No signals. No signs he made contact with anyone."

Luca nods. "Then we keep the watch. Rotate shifts. No gaps, no questions."

"Already in place," Matius says. "We've got eyes on every entrance. The tunnels. The alley. If someone even thinks about sniffing around here, we'll know."

Tomas glances toward the door again. "We'll take the next shift. Get some rest while you can."

I rub the ache from my shoulders, my heart still racing. Every creak in the stone, every whisper of wind outside, sets my nerves on edge. This place is our sanctuary and our prison now.

Luca finally settles against the cold stone wall, exhaustion pulling his limbs slack. His breathing evens out, slow and steady. I sit by his side, my eyes never leaving the main opening of the underground chamber.

Luca sleeps, and I think of how he carries too much. Too many scars, too many losses. I wonder how he still holds himself upright. How he still finds the strength to fight.

*He is nothing like Patrick.*

I realize thoughts of Patrick haven't crossed my mind in days. He feels like a distant memory compared to this man. Luca is braver, fiercer, tougher. He's more selfless, more courageous, and more considerate. He's just an all-around better person in ways that hit me harder than I expect.

As the night goes on, the familiar ache for my family returns. Their faces haunt me, the life I left behind slipping further away.

Here, I'm marked by my eyes, and I know the guards are hunting me. Fear tightens like a noose, whispering that this could be the end.

Still, I try to remind myself that I'm not helpless. For Luca, I'd do anything. His strength steadies me, even when the dark closes in and hope feels fragile.

The weight on my chest eases when Luca stirs beside me, blinking awake. He rubs his eyes, then looks over at me with a tired smile.

"Thanks for letting me sleep," he says quietly. "I needed it more than I realized."

I nod, smiling. "You definitely earned it."

He swings his legs off the bench and stands, stretching stiff muscles. "I'll check on the others, make sure no one's worse than we thought." He glances toward the corner where the others rest, some still bandaged and pale.

"Breakfast first, though," I say. "We all need strength for what's coming."

He grins. "Good idea."

"No one knows about this place. I mean, no guards showed up last night. That's a good sign."

Luca looks out the mouth of the cave, where dawn is bleeding into the sky. "Feels like the quiet before the storm." He steps closer. "You saved us," he says, his voice low. "That code, figuring out it was Ramón. If you hadn't...." He trails off, shaking his head.

"I didn't do it alone," I say quietly. "You helped, and you intercepted the note."

"Ava," he says, and the way my name hangs in the air between us makes my heart thrum hard enough to hurt. "I know this isn't the right time, but I need you to know before anything else happens—"

I hold still, terrified of what Luca's about to say.

"I love you. I didn't see it coming. It just happened—"

There's no space for fear in me anymore, not with him looking at me like that.

I step toward him. "I love you too," I whisper, the words catching in my throat, then rising stronger. "I didn't see it coming either, but I'd choose you. Again and again."

14

——————

# TEMPUS PRO REBELLIONEM

*LUCA*

SMOKE STILL HANGS over Toledo like a veil of judgment. Morning light pushes through it in streaks, golden and accusing. I move through the crooked alleyways with a dagger tucked in my boot and another strapped to my ribs beneath my tunic. The fire at the prison wasn't just destruction. It was a message.

Ramón had it lit to feed the chaos. He fanned the flames with oil and orders, and I'm sure he had help. Perhaps there are more of them, tucked inside the city like splinters under my skin. The thought curdles in my stomach.

I leave Ava at the bathhouse and head toward a small tavern I trust near the river's edge. The owner owes me a favor, or three, and I know she'll help without asking questions. The survivors from the prison need something warm in their bellies. Whatever I can carry back. It's the only thing I can do to help right now.

By the time I return, my arms are full with parcels of food wrapped in linen and steam still curling from the edges. The smell alone is enough to wake the dead. I just hope it's enough to remind the living that they made it through the night.

We eat in the ruins of the old bathhouse. The arches above us are fractured but still reach toward the sky like praying hands. The air is

87

damp and smells of ash, earth, and stone left to grieve. Our voices stay low, swallowed by the cavernous mikvah. It feels like a place that remembers sorrow, healing, and loss.

Ava brushes crumbs from her lap. "Do you think the guards will find this place?"

"If they do, the survivors won't be here," I murmur. "We'll move them soon, to one village at a time."

There's still soot under my fingernails from yesterday, and my lungs ache from the smoke. Yet when she looks at me, like she sees and accepts all of me, every jagged edge, I can almost forget the pain, if only for a moment. The bond between us is unmistakable.

I used to think love was something you offered, risked, and maybe lost, but saying the words aloud with her felt different. It was like she cracked something open in me, leaving a space that only she can fill.

After breakfast, we move carefully through the crumbling bath-house, stepping over broken tiles and shards of clay. Ava's cloak brushes against my arm as we walk side by side, and for a moment, the chaos outside feels far away.

"This place is bigger than I thought," she murmurs, glancing around. "Do you think there are more hidden rooms?"

I shrug, pretending casual curiosity, though my pulse quickens. "Perhaps. It's old enough that someone could have built secret passages that no living souls know of."

Her eyes light up, a spark of mischief and excitement I've missed. "Let's find out, then. Just a quick look around?"

I grin, nodding. "Quick," I say, winking. I already know we won't stop until we've explored every shadowed corner.

We step cautiously through the ruins, running hands over walls, examining nooks and faded frescoes. I notice a patch of stone at the far end of a corridor, slightly uneven, almost imperceptible. I press it lightly, then comes a soft click.

Ava straightens in an instant. The wall slides aside to reveal a narrow stairwell spiraling down into darkness. I look at her, waiting. "Shall we?"

She nods enthusiastically. "After you."

We descend carefully, each step groaning beneath us, dust puffing up around our boots. The air grows colder, and at the bottom, we enter a private chamber, half-collapsed, thick with dust, silent but for the whisper of our breathing. Light filters through cracks above, illuminating walls etched with intricate markings: Arabic, Hebrew, Latin. The carvings are sharp, reverent, stubbornly intact despite the years.

I trace one inscription with my fingers and read it aloud: *"Tempus pro rebellionem."* Time for rebellion.

Ava is close behind me, her warmth brushing my back. Close enough that I want to turn, to press my lips to hers in this secret place where the world feels paused.

"We should get back," she says.

"Yes." I nod, though neither of us moves right away. "They're probably wondering if we fell through the floor."

She bumps her shoulder into mine. "Come on."

We emerge from the stairwell without speaking, both of us carrying the gravity of what we just saw, and what it could mean for us. The survivors wait where we left them, huddled beneath the broken arches and faint shafts of morning light.

Ava bends to help a limping boy to his feet. "Should we move the people now or wait until nightfall?"

I glance around. "We'll take them through the narrow street behind the blacksmith now. It's safe."

She nods, and we guide them out in small clusters, avoiding main roads. The streets are still half-choked with ash and debris, but this part of the city hasn't stirred much yet.

By the time we reach the edge of Toledo, my shirt clings to my back. I slow beside Ava as the last of the group disappears down a wooded trail toward the village of Illescas.

She pulls her scarf off, fanning herself. "They'll be all right, won't they?"

"Yes, don't worry about them," I reply, wiping sweat from my jaw. "It's you we should be worried about."

Ava's eyes are still fixed on the trees, where the last survivor disappeared. "I could go back to Diego and Raquel's home?"

I hesitate. "Is that what you want?"

She glances at me, her lips pressed tight. "No. Not really, but it's the only thing that makes sense right now."

I want to tell her to stay with me. That we could make the ruins our home, our command post, our sanctuary, but her safety is worth more than my selfishness.

She sighs, then says, "First let's check on Abuela Maria."

I nod. "Of course. Let's go."

The walk to the old woman's home is quiet. Just the occasional call of birds, indifferent to the destruction around them.

When we reach her house, I knock, and Ava calls out softly. "Abuela Maria?"

A rustle, creak of wood, and a small figure appears in the doorway, wrapped in a shawl, gripping a wooden spoon.

"Ay, Dios mío," she gasps. "Ava!"

Ava rushes to her. They fold into each other, the kind of embrace that speaks more than words could. I hang back until Abuela Maria's watery eyes lift to me.

"And you," she says, her voice cracking. "I knew you wouldn't leave her."

"I tried. She's very stubborn. Just keeps following me around," I say with a wink.

"I have fresh pears and olives," the old woman offers. "You must eat something. You look like ghosts."

I glance at Ava. She gives me the tiniest nod.

"We'll eat," I say. "And then we'll figure out what's next."

After lunch, we help her carry water and organize supplies, blankets, jars of preserved fruit, and a small wooden box filled with useful tools. We tidy Abuela's little backyard, and for a while, it's easy to forget the chaos outside, and just be here, safe with her.

The road back to the bathhouse winds beneath our feet. Ava walks beside me, close enough that her shoulder brushes mine now and then. No guards follow.

I glance behind us one last time. Still clear. "We're good," I murmur. "No one's tailing us."

Ava gives a small nod, her eyes on me. "Then let's not waste time," she says, her voice tight.

"You don't have to go back to Diego's," I say. "We stayed at the bathhouse last night. No one knows we're there."

Ava looks up at me. "I'm so relieved to hear that," she admits softly. "I didn't want to leave you behind."

"If something happens," I add, "we're no good to each other if we're separated."

I don't want to let her go tonight, not after everything that's happened. We need time to untangle Ramon's reach, to figure out who he's influenced and how far it spreads. The bathhouse shows no sign of movement, no indication that we've been discovered. Relief washes over me, and for a moment, it feels like we've earned one more night, one more breath before everything ignites again.

I study her as we walk. I can't picture her gone from my side, not even for a short while. I reach for the door. "Let's just lie low," I say. "Rest, think, and plan."

The bathhouse is hushed when we slip inside, the stone still warm from the day's heat.

I see Luis and Martin, already waiting near the far wall, seated on a bench like they've been here a while. Their faces are drawn tight, unreadable.

"Something happened?" I ask before we're even close enough to sit.

Martin's already rising to his feet. "You'll want to see this."

Ava's shoulders stiffen. She doesn't speak, just lets me guide her forward.

Luis reaches into his coat and pulls out a folded parchment, then passes it to me.

"There's going to be a feast," he says. "In Aranjuez. Two nights from now."

I frown as I scan the paper. It is a formal invitation, not some casual letter. The names listed are high-ranking and dangerous.

"Noble families and military leaders," I say, my stomach tightening. "They're gathering like there's no blood on their hands. Where did you get this?"

Luis nods. "They're calling it a diplomatic restoration. A celebration of order. We stole it from Don Rodrigo de Velasco, our father's cousin."

"It'll be a gathering of snakes," Martin mutters. "Everyone will be drinking too much wine and speaking too freely. We need someone in the room. Someone who can listen without raising suspicion."

"Ava, we could go," I say. "You bear the look of a noblewoman, you own the gown, and I shall serve as your chaperone? None in that city know our names."

Martin looks at Ava. "You'd be surrounded. We'd position you with support nearby."

Ava straightens slowly, her shoulders drawn back and chin lifted. The fire in her eyes is no longer just defiance, but also filled with purpose.

"Then we'll go," she says, steady as stone. "Dress me in silk and call me a lady. I'll walk among wolves and smile like I belong."

She never ceases to astonish me. Not with her beauty–though God knows that alone could stop a man's heart–but with her courage. Every time I think I've seen the edge of her strength, she reveals a new depth. She should be afraid. Any sane person would be, but Ava meets danger like it's a dance she already knows the steps to with her quick mind, and unbreakable will.

I've seen noblewomen raised in courts with less poise. Soldiers with less steel in their spines. She doesn't just survive. Ava rises, unstoppable, again and again.

*Time for rebellion,* the wall had read. I think she was born for it.

# 15

# IMPOSTERS!

## *AVA*

THE WORDS ECHO in my mind–*I love you.*

Luca said them like a promise and a challenge wrapped into one. I haven't stopped turning them over in my mind since. He said he didn't mean to, and that it just happened… without even realizing the irony of his statement.

Of course, it *just happened.* I *just fell* through time from five hundred years in the future.

My heart races every time I think of it, and there's a fear tightening inside me. I'm falling for him faster than I should, maybe faster than I can bear, and the secret I carry feels heavier every time I look at him.

I think of the tarot card reader at the Renaissance Festival, of my cards, and the way she spoke of the fate of kingdoms, and love ruled by time. How could she have known? And how can I possibly explain it all to Luca?

I can't tell him who I really am when everything feels so fragile, so how could I have told him I love him? But I did, and I do. And yet he doesn't know I'm from another time, a future that's unimaginable to him. That truth could break everything between us, but part of me wants to trust him with it. Still, how do you tell someone you love that you're trapped in a past you don't belong to, and that every step you take could be borrowed time?

We left the ruins of the bathhouse early this morning and made our way back to Diego and Raquel's home. The place is quiet, familiar somehow already, and there I found my gown–the silk and lace that makes me feel like I could walk through the grandest halls without drawing suspicion.

Our next move is clear but risky. The feast is in Aranjuez, a gathering of nobles and soldiers. We can't just march in like a band of rebels, so we split up into pairs. Small enough to slip through shadows and blend with crowds, but strong enough to watch each other's backs.

Each group will take different routes and meet again in stages. First, at a small cottage tucked in the woods just outside the city, then outside the palace gates, in case we need backup.

I think about the others, allies, all bound by the same dangerous goal. Moving in small circles, crossing paths in different times, it feels like we're dancing on a knife's edge. Too many people together would draw eyes and questions we don't want. Too few, and we're vulnerable. But this way, we dilute the risk.

Luis and Martin left earlier to warn the rebellion empathizing family that lives in the cottage. It makes me feel safer knowing someone rode ahead and made arrangements.

The road winds through quiet farmland, and by the time the village comes into view, the tension in my chest finally starts to ease.

The cottage is stone and ivy-covered, tucked into the folds, nestled between wheat fields and hills. The place smells of rosemary, garlic, and baking bread long before we reach the door.

Luca knocks, and after a pause, the door opens just wide enough for a dark-eyed woman to peer out. She's older, with deep lines at the corners of her mouth and a cloth tied over her hair. Her gaze sweeps over us.

"Welcome!" she says, stepping aside. "My husband's in town with the miller, but he'll not speak a word of this. There's food warming and water for washing. Come in."

Luca gives a nod of gratitude as we step inside. Worn wooden beams line the ceiling, and herbs hang in bunches from pegs.

We don't speak much that first evening due to exhaustion, paranoia, and trying not to look like a pair of outlaws. We eat bread, dried figs, and meat too tough to chew, then curl up on pallets and furs on the floor. I wake once in the night and see Luca sitting against the door, his sword across his knees, watching. I wonder if this man ever sleeps.

By midmorning the next day, the others begin to arrive. Never more than a pair, six more men make their way to the cottage. Among them, Matius and Tomas, ready and deadly looking. The horses are led into the woods to be tethered beneath low branches.

The city's just over the ridge, barely a two-hour ride from here. We'll go before dark, and I'm supposed to look like I belong, so I slip into the back room with my satchel and take out the gown I made in 2025.

It's a rich ebony with gold embroidery winding up the sleeves and along the hem. I modeled it after the court styles I'd seen in museum exhibits and historical dramas, but made it practical enough to wear comfortably. The bodice laces up the back, and the neckline dips just low enough to be fashionable for the time but not scandalous. I worked on it for months, threading each tiny detail by hand, thinking I'd wear it to a Renaissance faire and maybe for Halloween. I never dreamed I'd wear it to a real Castilian castle in the fifteenth century.

My fingers tremble a little as I do my hair, half up in twists, the rest falling down my back in loose curls. I pinch my cheeks and draw in a deep breath.

When I open the door and step back into the main room, the noise halts.

Luca is standing near the fire, his arms crossed, deep in quiet conversation with Tomas. His eyes find mine, and everything else drops away.

His jaw slackens. The others blink and look again. I can feel heat rising into my cheeks.

"You look…." Luca begins speaking, then stops. I see longing and admiration cross his face.

I tuck a strand of hair behind my ear. "It'll do."

"It will bring kings to their knees," he says softly.

* * *

THE WAGON RATTLES OVER THE DIRT PATH, AND THE SUN IS JUST beginning to lower, casting streaks of pink and orange. I sit next to Luca, and I try to focus on anything besides the way he looks in that deep burgundy doublet with silver stitching that hugs his chest a little too perfectly. His dark hair is neatly combed, his face freshly shaved, and for the first time since I met him, he looks like the nobleman he keeps pretending not to be.

"You clean up well," I say, mostly to fill the silence, but also because I can't stop staring.

He smiles, slow and pleased. "Thank you, but I don't think any of them will believe that you are there with me. Are you nervous?"

I nod. "A little."

He leans forward and takes my hand in his. "You'll be the most beautiful woman there, and the most intelligent and brave by far."

His confidence in me is so immediate, so easy, that it almost undoes me. I don't know how I'm supposed to keep lying to someone who looks at me like that. So I just smile and squeeze his hand back.

When we round the last curve in the road, the city rises before us, white stone and slate rooftops catching the last of the daylight. The palace sits like a crown at the top of the hill, golden light glowing in the arched windows.

"We're right on time," Luca says.

I pull the invitation from the satchel tucked beside me. The names are neatly written in dark ink, noblemen, noblewomen, their houses and titles all listed out, but the important part is smudged. The name of the speaker, the one trying to persuade the court—no matter how we squint at it, the name is unreadable.

"We'll find out soon enough," I murmur as the wagon slows before the gates.

Inside the great hall, it's all candlelight and clamor. Tables are heavy with roasted meats, bread, fruit, and pitchers of wine. No one's paying attention to us, and that's a good thing. The nobles closest to the door are already deep in conversation, barely glancing up as we're ushered in by a servant in crisp green livery.

We walk side by side. I keep my chin high and my shoulders back like I belong here.

The steward at the dais looks up from his guest list. "Name?"

Luca doesn't miss a beat. "Don Rodrigo de Velasco. This is my wife, Lady Paloma."

The steward glances at the list, then nods once and gestures to a pair of empty seats halfway down the long table. "Welcome."

We are seated and no one gasps, screams, or shouts *imposters!* For now, we're safe. I pick up my goblet and take a long sip of wine.

The conversation around us swirls. Most of it's in Spanish, some in Latin. I catch snippets—*Granada, ships, royal charter, new routes*. We eat roasted duck, figs, and some kind of soft cheese with honey drizzled on top. Everything tastes incredible.

By the time the main course is cleared, I'm starting to think we might actually pull this off, and then a servant rings a bell.

"May I have your attention," the servant says, standing at the end of the table. "You have been summoned to hear a most esteemed speaker, a man whose vision could shape the future of our world."

A man stands from his seat near the head of the room. His dark beard is neatly trimmed, and his coat is black velvet.

"Ladies and gentlemen," he begins, his accent crisp but not quite Castilian, "I am honored to speak before you today. I come with maps, calculations, and a dream of reaching the Indies by sailing west. My name is Cristóbal Colón."

A sudden rush of lightheadedness hits me, and I almost faint.

Luca glances at me, concerned.

"Columbus. Fourteen ninety-two," I whisper. "Fourteen ninety-two."

Luca shifts beside me. "Ava?"

I try to slow my breathing, try to blink away the dizziness. I suddenly feel like my corset is laced too tight.

Luca leans in, his voice low. "Are you remembering something? Do you know him? Are you sure you're not—"

"I'm fine," I whisper, even though I'm not.

His eyes scan my face. "Are we going to get caught? If someone recognizes you—"

I feel as though my lungs have shut down, and I can't catch my breath. Fourteen ninety-two—it's the epicenter of everything I've studied. The Spanish Inquisition, the Crown's ruthless grip, the shadow of violence stretching across the land. Seeing Columbus here, now, makes it all terrifyingly real, and panic surges through me like wildfire.

Somehow, knowing the exact year I've fallen into is even more terrifying than being in the dark, and I wonder if I'll ever find my way home again.

# 16

# WHEN THE DANCE ENDS

## *AVA*

I MEET Luca's worried gaze and force a small smile. "It's fine. I know who Cristóbal Colón is, but I'm certain he doesn't know me. I'll tell you more later."

I settle beside Luca, brushing my fingers against his as I inhale deeply. He catches my eyes and smiles, comforting me.

As the speech winds down, the music swells. Couples rise to dance, the rustle of gowns and leather tapping against stone filling the hall.

Nearby, a cluster of men gossip, their voices loud enough to catch.

"The rebel who started the fire has been fattened well by the Crown's purse," one says, his eyes darting. "For two seasons he's fed us their secrets and plans."

Another scoffs, "No wonder the guards moved so swiftly last month. He's the holy officer's eyes inside Toledo."

A third mutters, "I heard the rebels caught wind and rolled his head."

I stiffen, glancing at Luca, who clenches his jaw.

"He was a traitor. What did he expect?" The first voice drunkenly spits out.

"There are more than him," the second replies. "There are others who are loyal to the holy officers, slipping through cracks they thought they sealed."

"And yet the rebels fight on," the third voice says, with what I can only assume is pity in his tone.

Luca leans closer to me. "This confirms it. Ramón had been tipping off the guards for at least two seasons before we even knew."

I nod, biting my lip, a pang of defeat curling in my chest. "Do you think anyone here suspects us?" I whisper.

He shakes his head. "We're ghosts tonight."

I let out a shaky breath and force a smile. "We need to keep listening."

We return to feasting, sipping wine and nodding politely as nobles debate matters of state and trade. Every sentence, every glance, could be a clue.

But over the hum of conversation, I keep catching the name *Francisco de Mendoza*, spoken low but often enough to make me curious.

I glance at Luca, watching how his facial expression changes to dread each time the name slips out of someone's mouth. He doesn't say anything, but I can tell it unsettles him.

Finally, I turn to Luca, lowering my voice. "Do you know who this Francisco de Mendoza is? They keep mentioning him."

Luca's eyes flash with irritation, and his voice drops drastically. "Yes. Francisco de Mendoza's a traitor—worse than Ramon ever was."

Luca's words hang between us, sharp and serious, but I don't fully understand what it means yet. Whatever Francisco de Mendoza has done, it sounds dangerous, but now isn't the time to ask questions. We're still surrounded by people, and drawing attention would be foolish. I tuck the thought away, knowing it's something we'll have to revisit later when we're safe.

As the evening winds down, we slip quietly from the hall, hearts pounding with what we've learned and what's still unknown.

Our wagon waits in the shadowed courtyard. I climb in beside Luca, the chilled night air rushing in as the horses start their slow journey back through the darkened countryside.

From the edge of the village, I see shadowy figures, our guards, scattered at careful distances, keeping watch. They ride silently, protectors in the night.

Luca finds my hand again. "We've gained more than we lost tonight."

I squeeze his hand. "But the fight just got harder. How will we ever figure out who among our group are traitors?"

"I don't know yet, but we'll have to act soon," Luca says with a worried expression.

The trip back seems longer than the journey to the city. Luca sits close, his hand now resting lightly on my knee. The world fades to a blur of trees and soft moonlight.

He turns to me with his eyes narrowed in curiosity. "Now, you must tell me, how did you know the explorer, Cristóbal Colón?"

I swallow hard, scrambling for the right words, even though I've been rehearsing my answer to this exact question in my head all night. "I don't know him personally, but I've heard of him, and it triggered a memory. His name just caught me off guard, that's all." I try to sound casual, and it seems like Luca buys it.

"You know, you're far too beautiful," Luca says softly, "to go all night without dancing."

I blush. "Thank you, but I don't know if I remember how to dance."

He chuckles, low and warm. "Then we find somewhere quiet, and I'll teach you. Just for a moment."

I nod, unable to resist. The wagon slows as we reach a narrow path veering off the main road. Luca signals our guards to give us some privacy as the horses roll us into a small clearing.

Olive trees crowd the edges, their silver leaves shimmering faintly in the moonlight. The grove smells sweet, earthy, and wild.

Luca steps down first, reaching his hand to me. I take it, and he helps me out of the wagon, pulling me close. He removes my boots first and then his own, and we dance barefoot on the grass.

He moves with surety, leading me into a slow, easy dance. Our feet shift lightly as Luca hums a ballad, his gentle touch making my heart pound loud enough to drown out the distant sounds of the night. For a moment, the fear, the secrets, the rebellion—all of it fades.

"I've never met anyone like you before," he murmurs against my temple.

"I can say the same of you," I whisper back, and it's true.

We move together beneath the stars, and when the dance ends, Luca presses a soft kiss to my forehead, pulling me even closer. Every touch from him sets me on fire. I never imagined a moment like this could exist, especially not here, or now.

His eyes catch mine, dark and unyielding, and I see everything there—strength, longing, a promise I don't dare say aloud but feel in every heartbeat.

He leans in, pressing his lips to mine, tentative at first, as if asking permission without words. I give it freely as his hands trace the curve of my waist, pulling me impossibly close.

Time slows, the world narrowing to the softness of his kiss. We move together toward the trees for more covering. Luca leans me beneath the olive branches, the rough bark pressing behind me. His fingers slide across the bodice of my gown, sending a shiver straight to my core. Every nerve is alive, every sense sharp and electric.

Luca kisses me slowly as his hands work at the ties of my gown. The fabric loosens and slips from my shoulders like a waterfall. Luca watches me lust in his gaze. I reach for him, and in one smooth motion, he undresses, shedding everything between us.

He lowers me gently onto a blanket of meadow grass. Luca's hands never leave me, exploring my every curve with passion.

His name tumbles from my lips in a whisper, half-gasp, half-plea. Luca settles between my legs, his body warm, his mouth everywhere —at my throat, my breasts, up and down my thighs. He worships every inch of me like I'm something he's only ever dreamed of.

His hand slips lower, parting me with fingers both gentle and hungry. My back arches instinctively, tilting my hips toward him, aching for more. I can't form words. I just moan.

"You're perfect," he murmurs, voice thick with lust. "Tell me what you want."

"You," I breathe. "Now. Please."

As Luca guides himself into me with a slow thrust, I gasp. He's thick, filling me deliciously. I clutch his shoulders, and he groans low in his throat.

We move together. He drives deeper, harder, and every thrust receives a moan from my lips. I wrap my legs around him, pulling him closer, needing him to stay, to never leave.

Pleasure builds sharp and bright in my belly, coiling tighter and tighter until it bursts. I cry out, my fingers digging into his back, shaking with the force of my climax. Luca follows with a growl, his hips stuttering as he comes, spilling into me.

Luca lies beside me, one arm wrapped around my waist. His breath is warm against my shoulder, his thumb tracing slow circles on my skin.

I don't know how I ended up here, undressed in the grass with a man born five hundred years before me, but there's no part of me that wants to leave his arms. I've never belonged in his world, and yet, somehow, in this quiet place, I feel more like myself than I ever have.

17

# CODES AND SYMBOLS

## *LUCA*

WE'RE BACK at the cottage, the room dim and warm from the dying fire. Outside, the night hangs heavy and silent, broken only by the steady watch of our guards, spread out beneath the ancient oaks. Their soft footsteps and low whispers seep through the thin wooden walls, a constant reminder that danger still lurks just beyond our fragile shelter.

I lie beside Ava on the woven blanket, her breath evening out now in sleep, but my mind won't calm. The night, the feast, the dancing beneath the moon, and the way she moved with such grace and fire, replay over and over. Most of all, I remember the way she felt beneath my hands, the heat of her skin, the softness and strength of her body pressed close to mine. Making love with her for the first time was a passionate reckoning, and a promise.

And yet, as those tender memories flood me, my heart drops when the name of Francisco de Mendoza creeps in. The traitor's name was whispered too often tonight and too close to home. I've dealt with men like him before, serpents wearing masks, slipping poison into trusted circles. That level of betrayal cuts deeper because it feels personal, a wound that hasn't yet scabbed over.

I shift, careful not to wake Ava, and stare into the flames. How can

I protect her when threats gather like storm clouds on the horizon? How can I keep her safe in a world where loyalty is a fragile, fleeting thing? No matter the battles ahead, I'll fight for her.

Sleep finally pulls at my eyelids, and I let it take me.

* * *

THE ROAD STRETCHES OUT BEFORE US AS THE SUN CLIMBS HIGHER, casting light over the trees lining our path. The horses move briskly, and Ava rides beside me.

By the middle of the second day, we reach the bathhouse, the hidden place our allies gather. The air is filled with cautious relief as familiar faces emerge from the shadows. Each of them was called to the base by messengers, spies, and other rebels. Each of them is here because they want justice.

I stand before them, the gravity of what I'm about to say heavy on my chest. They watch, expectant, waiting for news. I take a deep breath and begin.

"At the feast held in Aranjuez, I overheard Francisco de Mendoza's name more than once." I watch their faces carefully. Some stiffen, and others exchange quick, knowing glances.

"Francisco de Mendoza was Ramon's superior, and he's the real traitor." As I continue, a murmur runs through the room, subtle but certain. "He lives in darkness, protected by guards, nobles, even the royals. His reach is long, his lies deep. He's been sending agents into rebel meetings, feeding information straight to the enemy."

Heads nod around me, confirmation in their eyes. Francisco de Mendoza is a name that carries weight, one soaked in betrayal and bloodshed.

"He's the spider at the center of this web, the one pulling strings." I pause, letting my words sink in. "Mendoza is still out there. He's the one we need to find. I want his bloodshed."

The room tightens, energy shifting from cautious hope to simmering resolve. A few hands grip weapons. A few eyes harden with the taste of revenge.

One of our scouts, a lean man, steps forward. "We've heard whispers, footsteps in the dark, men moving where they shouldn't. Mendoza's men are clever. They don't show themselves unless they're sure."

"That's why we must be shrewd," I say. "We can't afford mistakes. Mendoza's protection makes him dangerous, but not untouchable. We find him, we end this."

Tomas speaks up. "The traitor won't hide forever. When he shows himself, we'll be ready."

"Trust no one. Watch each other's backs, and keep your ears open. Every word, every movement matters," Matius adds.

The meeting breaks with a sense of purpose, the tension easing but not disappearing. I catch Ava's eye, and she gives me a small smile.

"How can I help?" she asks, her voice barely above the conversation around us.

I glance at Matius and Tomas, who stand nearby, already deep in thought about our next moves.

Matius raises an eyebrow. "You're good with codes and symbols?" he asks.

Ava nods. "I am. What are you thinking?"

Tomas, always practical, speaks next. "Information is our lifeline. If Mendoza's spies are everywhere, we need a way to communicate that they can't intercept or understand."

I step forward. "A code. Something only we understand. Ava, do you think you can create that?"

She meets my gaze without hesitation. "I can devise a system simple enough to learn quickly but complex enough to fool anyone who were to intercept it."

"That would give us an edge," Matius says approvingly.

"I'll start right away," Ava says, determination in her voice.

Tomas and Matius quickly return with supplies for Ava, their arms loaded with scraps of parchment, charcoal sticks, and a handful of quills.

Ava's eyes light up as she takes the materials from them, undoubtedly already thinking ahead. She spreads the parchment carefully across a flat stone slab, smoothing the edges. Her fingers move with quiet confidence, unrolling the possibilities hidden in blank sheets.

"We need something simple enough to memorize, but complicated enough to fool Mendoza's men," she explains. "A mix of substitution and symbols. Letters replaced by shapes or marks that don't look like letters at all. Then we add a key, something only we understand."

I watch her, feeling more impressed by the second. Ava is brilliant, quick, and fearless.

She quickly sketches out a few shapes, then assigns letters to each one. "We'll need to practice so it becomes second nature."

The four of us take turns memorizing the code. I repeat the shapes and letters aloud, Tomas scribbles a quick note, and Matius watches for mistakes. Ava leads us, her patience endless as she explains each symbol's meaning.

"Think of it like a dance," she says softly, "where every step has a purpose and timing is everything."

I grin at her metaphor. Only Ava would turn secret codes into something poetic.

Hours pass, but no one tires. The urgency keeps us focused, with every mistake corrected, every symbol practiced until it flows naturally.

By the time the first pale light creeps through a cracked window, we've written and decoded several messages. The code isn't perfect, but it's ours, a shield against the evil that stalks us.

I meet Ava's gaze, seeing the fierce satisfaction there. "You did this," I tell her. "This will save lives."

She shrugs, a faint smile playing on her lips. "We all did."

Matius claps me on the shoulder. "Now, that's something worth staying up until dawn for."

Tomas stretches, fatigue finally setting in. "We'll need to teach the others soon. Mendoza won't wait."

I nod, my heart pounding with a mix of exhaustion and hope. This code is more than symbols on parchment. It's our weapon, and with Ava leading, we just might stand a chance.

# 18

# I PROMISE



I NEVER IMAGINED I'd find such fierce purpose in something as simple as a code, but sitting in this ancient, abandoned bathhouse, surrounded by scraps of parchment with charcoal-stained fingers, I felt alive in a way I hadn't before. Crafting that secret language for our group wasn't just a task. It was a weapon, a lifeline, a sliver of hope in the shadowed world we live in.

Tomas, Matius, and Luca took to it quickly, their sharp minds eager to absorb every symbol and substitution I devised. We practiced until the shapes and sounds became second nature, until the code flowed from their fingers like a secret song only they could hear. They carried it not on paper, but locked safely in their minds, a living cipher that no enemy could steal or decipher. No written proof to fall into Mendoza's hands, and no trail to follow.

The men teach the code to some of the messengers who left with it and scatter it like sparks across Toledo and neighboring villages, each man a bearer of our invisible thread, our link to one another. Through bustling market squares and quiet forest paths, through whispers in crowded taverns and messages slipped between trusted allies, our code grows into an unseen web of resistance.

It means we can plan, warn, and fight without fear that betrayal will tear us apart, especially when it comes to ending Francisco de Mendoza's reign of poison. I feel the weight of that mission settling into my bones. We're no longer just rebels. We're a network, a force threaded together by trust and cunning.

When Luca tells me he's leaving on a quick mission with Tomas, a small knot of worry twists in my stomach.

"I'll be right back," he promises.

I want to believe him, but fear lurks beneath hope like a shadow. Still, I nod, biting back the urge to insist he stay.

He steps closer. "You're the reason we have this edge." His voice is low, a comfort against the anxiety stirring inside me. "I'll be back soon. Don't go anywhere."

"I'll be here. I promise."

As they head out, dust kicking up behind them, I stand alone amidst the cracked stone and empty pools of the bathhouse. The silence presses in, but it's not empty. It hums with purpose, with the promise of secrets safe and plans yet to unfold.

The code I made isn't just ink and shapes. It's a symbol of what we fight for, the chance to protect each other, to outwit the darkness that threatens to swallow us whole.

The hours stretch on. I try to focus on anything other than my worries, but every shadow seems to lengthen, and every noise seems louder in the stillness.

Suddenly, the door creaks open, and Luis and Martin step inside, their faces grave. "Abuela Maria is hurt," Luis says quietly. "The holy officers came through again. She was standing up for a child they were torturing. They beat her badly." My heart lurches. "She called out for help when they left, and Catalina heard her. She sent word to us."

Martin nods. "Abuela wants to see you. She insisted we come get you." Without hesitation, I grab my cloak and follow them into the darkening streets, my mind racing with worry and determination.

We hurry through narrow alleys to Catalina's house, the terror of the news clawing at my chest. When we arrive, Catalina is already tending to Abuela Maria, who sits slumped in a wooden chair, bruises blooming dark across her cheek and swollen lips parted in shallow breaths. Her eyes brighten faintly when she sees me.

"Ava," she croaks, voice rough. "Thank you for coming."

I kneel beside her, carefully wiping the drying blood from her face. "You're safe now," I whisper.

She winces but manages a weak smile. "That child… they had no right. Someone has to stand up for the little ones." Her spirit remains unbroken, even if her body is battered.

Catalina fetches water and helps me settle Abuela Maria more comfortably. We exchange sorrowful glances.

Hours pass. Luis and Martin return to the streets, teaching the code to only the most trusted allies. Eventually, Maria asks if I'll help her get home to go to sleep in her own bed. I stand and reach for her hand, and she uses my arm as leverage to rise to her feet.

I help support her fragile frame as we step carefully down the street. Every movement sends a shudder through her, but her grip tightens around my arm with quiet determination. "I'm stronger than I look," she mutters with a faint smile, though her eyes betray the exhaustion beneath.

I guide her inside her house, settling her gently into her bed.

"You did the right thing," I tell her softly, brushing damp strands of hair from her face. "No one deserves that kind of cruelty."

She nods, her eyes heavy with pain and gratitude. "We have to speak up for the meek."

Hours pass as I tend to her wounds, wrapping bandages and brewing a simple tea from herbs Abuela Maria insists will help soothe her aches. She drinks her tea and not long after, her eyelids flutter closed.

As the night deepens, I remember I promised Luca I would be at the bathhouse when he returned. If I'm not there, he'll worry, and I didn't even leave a note.

I slip quietly through the door, the cool night air wrapping around me as I step onto the deserted street. The moon casts its pale light on the cobblestones, but shadows crowd the corners, swallowing everything beyond reach.

My footsteps echo softly as I make my way back toward the bath-house, my heart pounding louder with every step.

A huge hand clamps over my mouth without warning, stifling my scream before it can escape. Another hand presses a coarse sack down over my head, blinding me instantly. Panic surges, my muscles tensing, but I'm dragged backward, my feet stumbling on uneven stones.

I struggle against the unseen grip, but the darkness and the strength of the man dragging me along make it impossible to break free. My mind races.

*Who could this be? What do they want? And how do I get free?*

# 19

## WHERE IS SHE?

### *LUCA*

THE DARK STREETS are quiet when I reach the bathhouse. Tomas walks at my side, still flushed with excitement from teaching Ava's code. Her idea is catching on faster than I dared hope, but we teach it only to the most loyal rebels who have earned our trust.

I push the door open, expecting the familiar creak, the faint steam, the murmur of voices. Instead, silence greets me. No lamplight, no rustle of cloth. The stone floor is cool under my boots as I step inside, scanning the shadows.

"Ava?" My voice echoes too loudly.

No answer.

I walk through each chamber, my heart knocking harder with every step. The benches are empty.

Tomas frowns. "Where is she?"

"I don't know." My tone comes out sharper than I intend. I take a slow breath and force my mind to calm. "Check the streets. Ask around. See if anyone's seen her tonight."

He nods and disappears into the dark.

Alone, I search. I look for overturned baskets, scraps of parchment, anything. I trace the floor with my eyes for scuff marks, broken pottery, blood.

Nothing.

My thoughts turn darker. Did she leave in a hurry? If so, why didn't she send word? She knows I'd follow. Or worse, did someone take her?

I stand in the center of the bathhouse, the sound of my breathing loud in my ears. I hate waiting, but I force myself to stay. If she comes back, I want to be here.

Time stretches.

Finally, footsteps in the corridor. Two figures emerge from the shadows, Luis and Martin.

"Luca," Luis says, a note of concern in his voice. "We were looking for you."

"What's wrong?"

"It's Abuela Maria," Martin answers quickly. "She was beaten by a guard. She's resting now, but she's hurt."

A ripple of worry moves through me. "Is she all right?"

"She'll recover," Luis says. "Ava went to help her."

The tight knot in my chest doesn't loosen. Of course, Ava would go to Maria. She's always the one to protect others, no matter the cost, but the thought of Maria beaten, her body bruised for standing up to those monsters, stabs through me like a knife.

"Come on. We have to get to her," I growl, already moving toward the door.

I cross the village quickly, the first pale hint of dawn softening the sky. The streets smell of baking bread now, ovens just lit for the morning.

When I reach Abuela Maria's house, I knock once before stepping inside. "Ava?"

Silence.

Abuela Maria sleeps soundly in her bed, a damp cloth over her forehead, but the chair beside her is empty.

I search the small home, each room quieter than the last. No Ava, and no note.

The sun edges higher, painting the windows gold, and dread slides cold through my veins.

*Where is she?*

By the time the sun is high, my pace has turned into a near-run. Every corner I turn, I expect to see her, tugging her hood lower, slipping into shadow, but the streets give me nothing.

I circle back to the bathhouse just in case she somehow slipped past me, but it's as empty as I left it. The basin water is cold. Her satchel isn't there.

My mind claws at explanations, none of them good. I send Matius to check the north quarter, and to double back through the old well road. I take the south, cutting through narrow lanes where laundry flaps like surrender flags above me.

At the end of the third street, I see two holy officers dragging a man by his collar. He stumbles once, twice, then disappears around the bend. No one dares watch too closely. I force myself to keep walking, though my pulse is hammering.

Every instinct tells me I'm running out of time. I lean against a wall, scanning every face that passes. I picture her bound, silenced, taken to one of the cells beneath the castle. The thought digs its claws into me and refuses to let go.

As the sun sets, I've made my decision. I send runners in pairs with a place and a time. The wine cellar beneath Suarez's tavern is perfect. The smell of fermenting barrels covers the scent of too many people in one place, and the noise upstairs drowns out low voices.

When I arrive, the first few are already there. A handful more slip in after, their faces tight with unease. The cellar's lantern light throws long shadows against the damp stone walls, making us all look like ghosts.

"Keep your voices down," I say, pacing the narrow space. "If Ava's missing, it's not just her. It's the code, the network, every connection we've built. We treat the bathhouse as burned until we know otherwise."

Murmurs pass between them, but no one argues. They've seen enough to know I'm not overreacting.

"We split our routes. No one walks alone; no one uses the same path twice. We move messages by code, and if any of you are approached by guards, by priests, you say nothing. You hear me?"

Heads nod in the dim light. The air feels heavy, thick with the weight of what's unsaid.

I'm about to assign shifts when the door at the top of the stairs creaks. Every head turns. Boots thump down the steps, and a messenger boy appears, breathing hard.

He finds me instantly, his gaze sharp. "They've got her."

The words hit like a blade. "Who? How do you know? What did you see, boy?"

"Your woman," he says, swallowing hard. "Taken in the middle of the night. Black robes. Not by the city guard, but by the holy officers. I saw them grab her, and I followed them. She's in chains in the holding compound outside the east gate."

The cellar goes silent. I can feel every eye on me, waiting.

"How did you find me here?" I ask.

"I heard rumors of where you'd meet tonight. I've been trying to find you all day, Luca." His voice is small now.

For a moment, the lantern light blurs. I press my palms flat against the table, forcing my voice to stay level. "When?"

"Before dawn. They kept it quiet. No trial. No crowd."

My jaw locks. Quiet means they want her for themselves. Interrogation, maybe worse, and they'll move her to the fortress beneath the palace if we wait.

The cellar is filled with tension. I spread the crude sketch of the holding compound out on the table, my hands braced on its edges.

"We know where she is," I say, my voice quiet but stern. "In chains outside the east gate. It's not heavily fortified, but the priests and holy officers patrol it constantly. No guards answer to anyone but them."

A silence follows. Luis rubs his chin, his eyes narrowing. "We can't just storm the place. Too many of them, and they're ruthless."

Martin's voice cuts in, his tone sharp. "We need a distraction. Something big enough to pull them away, even if just for minutes."

I nod. "Minutes could be enough. But what?"

A rustle from the far corner. Tomas steps forward, his fingers twitching. "What about the livestock? The Crown's prized animal. They keep them close, but if they got loose, the whole guard would scramble to catch them."

A spark of interest spreads.

"Like horses?" Matius asks, voice cautious.

"More than that," Tomas says. "The royal stables hold more than horses. Bulls, goats, sheep, and even a few prized dogs. If we could get them out, stampede through the streets, the guards would be chasing animals instead of us."

Luis shakes his head, skeptical. "That's risky. The stables are guarded too."

"But not as tightly as the prison," I say. "And the animals are valuable, worth more than any one guard's life. They'll send every available man to round them up."

Martin taps the map. "While the city's in chaos, Luca slips in, unchains Ava, and we get her out."

"Tomas and Matius, could you escort her to safety?" Luis asks, looking to them.

Tomas nods. "My abuelo lives in Guadamur. It's a quiet place, friendly to the cause. We could get her there."

"It's a narrow window," I say, my hands pressing harder on the table. "If the holy officers move her before we act, we lose her for good."

Luis adds, "We'll have lookouts posted, eyes on every approach. If something goes wrong, we pull back immediately."

I pace a slow circle. "We can't afford mistakes. No loose ends."

Tomas looks to me with urgency in his eyes. "We can't just wait. If we do nothing, they'll kill her."

I nod again, my heart pounding. "All right. We prepare for the livestock. Tomas and Matius secure the escape route. Luis and Martin, get the men ready. We move at dusk."

Luis grins, despite the pressure of it all. "We'll need to know the guard shifts, the stable entrances, and the best way in and out."

"Exactly," I say. "We gather every scrap of information we can. We'll meet here again before nightfall. This is our chance to save her. If we don't get her out now, we won't be able to save her at all."

We all know the risks, but the cost of failure is too high.

"Let's get to work."

20

# CHASING THEIR DINNER

## *AVA*

THE ROPES BITE into my wrists until my fingers tingle. I can't move them, but the pain is sharp enough to remind me I'm still alive, for now. The air reeks of sweat and iron, the sickly sweet tang of blood hanging in it like a warning. My knees ache from the dirt-packed floor, but I don't dare move. Any movement draws their eyes, and I've had enough of their eyes.

They know who I am. I see it in the smirks, the too-long glances, the muttered words that hit me like stones. One soldier leans against the wall, his arms folded, and says to the others, "That's her, the one who sang that crazy song, kept us looking the wrong way while the gates were opened."

Another spits on the floor near my feet. "She thought we wouldn't find out she was working with the rebels."

The first man grins without humor. "You're not clever, girl. Just lucky, and luck runs out."

One of them steps closer, his boots pounding the dusty floor, his shadow swallowing me. He doesn't touch me, not yet, but his gaze crawls over me like ants under my skin. "Maybe we'll hang you. Maybe we'll keep you for... other things first." His eyes trail deliberately down my body. "We'll see."

I tell myself not to cry. Not here, where they'll take it as an invitation to be even more cruel. But my eyes sting, and my body shakes anyway.

Footsteps echo outside the door. I know when the hinges groan open that it's the officer who caught me. He is taller than the others, with the cold composure of someone who could slit your throat without spilling a drop on his polished boots.

He studies me for a long moment, then crouches so we're eye to eye. "You've made quite the mess," he says, spitting out the words. "That little performance of yours cost me half my guard detail. A distraction, but a costly one."

My stomach turns to ice.

"How many lives did you save?" he asks. "Ten? Twenty? Do you even know? You opened the gates for them. You helped them vanish into the hills. And you thought we'd never find you? We have eyes and ears all over the city, and you don't necessarily fit in around here, woman. I wonder if you'll break quickly or fight. I like the ones who fight."

Just then, the captain walks up, barking orders and threats about work to do and no time for standing around flirting with prisoners.

When they finally leave, I stay on the ground, trying to catch my breath. My wrists throb, and my shoulder burns where one of them shoved me. I press myself into the corner, trying to make my body smaller.

The ache in my jaw reminds me of his fingers gripping my face, the way his nails bit into my skin. I rub it with my shoulder, but it doesn't help. My pulse hasn't slowed. My mouth still tastes of copper.

For a moment I think about the gallows, about the clean drop of a rope compared to… this. Death is simple. This isn't.

Boots approach again. My stomach knots. I draw my knees up, curling into myself, bracing for the door to open. The latch rattles—then stops. Voices murmur on the other side. I hear a crude laugh, then the sound of footsteps moving away.

Relief seeps in, leaving me weaker than before. They'll be back. I know they will, and next time, I might not be saved by a shipment or a captain's temper.

I drag my bound hands to my lap and flex my fingers, wincing at the stab of returning circulation. Rope fibers scrape my skin. I imagine them fraying and breaking, anything to give me a chance to run, but the knots are too tight.

Somewhere outside, a cart creaks and a gate slams shut. Life goes on in the prison compound, with soldiers going about their orders while I sit here, waiting for whatever comes next.

My chest won't stop tightening. I try to slow my breathing, but every inhale is too sharp, every exhale too fast. I can't tell if minutes or hours have passed since they left. The shadows in the room look exactly the same. Maybe it's been days.

I don't know where Luca is. I don't know if he's even alive. The last time I saw him, I promised I would be at the bathhouse when he returned.

A cold wave rolls through me, heavier than the ropes around my wrists. I was born in 1996, and I'm going to die in 1492....

I think of my sister, Eden, her quick laugh, the way she always knows exactly what to say to make me feel less alone. My parents, who must be frantic by now—weeks without a word, no messages, no calls. They don't live nearby anymore, and I left the nest years ago, but I know they're searching, praying, wondering if I'm alive.

I miss my colleagues, the familiar hum of the lecture hall, and the spark in the students' eyes when a new idea finally clicks. I miss the smell of old books and coffee, the endless stack of papers to grade, the comforting routine of my job as a professor.

I close my eyes and hold on to those memories like a lifeline. If I forget who I am, who I was, then what's left to fight for?

Nothing has made sense since that day at the Renaissance fair. The dizzying, bone-jarring pain when I fell in the water and hit my head.

When I woke up here.

If magic, time travel, or quantum physics brought me to 1492, it has to be able to take me back, right? Maybe it's the Tagus River. Maybe Ferdinand and Isabella's palace is the portal.

If I could get back there, if I could jump in again, maybe I'd wake up in 2025. I try to imagine the path from here to there. I don't even know where "here" is, not exactly. The guard blindfolded me before taking me to this compound and didn't take it off until I was inside, so I don't know what path to take to escape, even if I could break free.

The walls feel closer. My wrists ache, and I pull at the ropes until they burn. My pulse is in my ears, my vision spotted at the edges.

Then the floor shifts.

It's slight at first, but then it comes again, stronger. The stones under me tremble, a low, shuddering groan rising from deep in the earth. Dust drifts down from the ceiling in soft gray spirals. It feels like an earthquake.

I've read about them happening here in Toledo—some in the Middle Ages, maybe one in the eighteenth century. I can't remember the dates, but the sensation is unmistakable. The same deep, rolling sway I felt in California once, when I was visiting my cousin and the ground began to move.

The shaking doesn't stop. It grows. A clatter of voices shouts over each other outside, boots pounding in every direction. Something huge crashes outside.

The door bursts open. For a split second, I think it's the guards who left me here, coming back to finish what they started, but then I see him.

"Luca!" I nearly shout.

He's already moving, a knife in his hand. "Quiet," he says, breathless. In two swift motions, the blade slices through the ropes at my wrists. My arms fall forward, tingling and numb, but free. He hauls me to my feet. "We have to go. Now."

We slip into the hall, keeping low. Shouts echo from every direction, but no one's looking at us. They're all running toward the main gates. Outside, the sun stings my eyes after the dim cell.

Tomas and Matius wait by the side wall, both armed, both watching the chaos in the courtyard. The sound hits me first—screams, and the pounding of hooves.

Then I see them.

Goats, sheep, horses, chickens, cattle, even two massive oxen, all scattering in every direction. Soldiers lunge for reins and feathers, slipping in the dirt. The captain trips over a goat and lands flat on his back. Feathers drift through the air like snow.

"What—?" My voice cracks. "What is going on?"

Tomas grins, grabbing my arm to keep me moving. "We let every last animal in the castle herds loose," he says. "Seemed like the quickest way to cause trouble."

"While they're chasing their dinner," Matius adds, "we're getting you out of here."

We sprint down a narrow lane toward a gap in the wall, and Luca never lets go of my hand. Behind us, the compound is in chaos. Shouts of "Close the gates!" mixing with the wild calls of frightened animals. My heart is still hammering, but now it's not just fear. It's adrenaline.

When we reach the outskirts, we don't stop running until the noise fades to a distant roar. Only then do we slow, gasping for breath.

I turn to Luca, Tomas, and Matius, and for a moment, I can't find words. In all my life, in any century, I've never met men this loyal and brave. They risked everything for me.

I swallow hard, my eyes stinging again, but this time with something warm. "Thank you," I whisper.

Luca squeezes my hand. "You'd do the same for us."

And the terrifying truth is—I would.

21

# THIS NIGHT IS OURS

## *AVA*

Tomas and Matius kept four horses hidden, and now we ride hard, weaving through thick woods beyond the city walls.

I can barely believe I'm free. After everything–the ropes, the threats, the pain and terror–I'm alive and moving toward something that feels like safety.

Tomas leads us down a narrow dirt road lined with olive trees, the moon casting light on the path ahead. "My abuelo's house isn't far," he says. "We'll be safe there until morning."

When we reach the village, it's quiet, small, almost forgotten by the rest of the world. The houses are simple, stone and wood, worn by years of wind and sun.

A beautiful young woman greets us at the doorway of a modest house. Tomas introduces her as his cousin, Samira, and quietly explains to her the danger we're in.

"Abuelo is resting," she says. "You're welcome here."

Samira invites us to sit and soon brings over steaming cups of tea. The fire warms the room, and the tea settles my stomach. Luca stays beside me, his face tense and guarded, like all of us, on edge and exhausted.

Safe doesn't mean healed, and fear still clings to me, my mind racing with everything I haven't told Luca.

I can't keep hiding. When morning comes, I'll tell Luca the truth about who I am and where I came from.

* * *

TOMAS AND SAMIRA MOVE QUIETLY, PREPARING A SIMPLE BREAKFAST OF bread, eggs, olives, and strong black coffee. Outside, birds sing, and the village slowly wakes beneath a stunningly clear blue sky.

When the meal ends, I clear my throat. "Luca... is there somewhere we can speak privately?"

Tomas cuts in, "There's a garden if you go out through the back door. It's peaceful."

Luca nods, standing and offering me a hand. We walk through the back door into a small garden where blossoms spill over a trellis, and he leads me to a shaded nook with a comfortable sofa, worn but inviting. The air smells of jasmine, a calm contrast to the storm inside me.

I sit, my hands folded tightly in my lap, and look up at him. His eyes hold something like hope, and wariness.

"I need to tell you something," I begin, my voice low. "Something I haven't said before."

He leans forward, silent.

"I lied," I admit. "Not about everything, but about the most important part. I never had memory loss. I always knew who I was."

Luca's brow furrows, his concern deepening.

"I was afraid," I admit, "afraid of how you'd react. Afraid you'd think I was insane."

He reaches out as if to touch my hand, but stops himself. "I don't understand, Ava. What do you mean?"

"What I'm about to say–" I hesitate. "It probably won't sound believable. It barely sounds believable to me."

Luca's eyes narrow, waiting.

"I traveled through time," I say, the words tasting strange and impossible on my tongue. "I'm from the year 2025."

He wrinkles his forehead, stunned. I can see the gears turning in his mind, trying to make sense of it, trying not to dismiss it outright.

"How can any of this be true?" he asks, his voice rough. "Why should I believe you? How do I know you're not just… broken from what you've been through?"

I meet his gaze, steadying myself. "I don't expect you to believe me right away. I only want the chance to prove it."

Luca looks at me like I've lost my mind. "A time traveler? That's a lot to take in, Ava. How am I supposed to believe something like that?"

"I know it sounds crazy, but think back to the feast the other night."

He raises an eyebrow.

"I wasn't just nervous or scared. I know who Cristóbal Colón is, and more than that, I know what he's going to do."

Luca frowns, trying to follow. "What do you mean?"

"He's going to sail west and claim lands that don't belong to him. He'll say he 'discovered' America, but there were already millions of people living there. His arrival starts a whole wave of colonization—suffering for the people there."

He shakes his head, overwhelmed. "So you're saying you come from a time after all this has happened?"

I nod. "Yes. In the year 2025, I'm a history professor. I teach classes about your time and everything that's going on here and now. That's how I recognized Cristóbal Colón."

I take a deep breath, meeting his eyes. "There's more. The bathhouse… that was me. I sent the message telling you it was there."

Surprise flashes across Luca's face. "You? But why keep it secret?"

"I couldn't tell you before. I was afraid you'd call me a lunatic or a witch. I didn't know how you'd react, but I needed you to know. I wanted to help."

He lets out a slow breath. "There's so much to take in…."

"I know, and I'm so sorry I lied to you, Luca. But it's true. I'm from the future. That's why I am so good at cracking and developing codes. I studied the codes from your era."

"What does this mean for us? For you? Are you able to travel back home? Do you want to, Ava?" he asks, his eyes brimming with tears.

I stare down at my lap, the gravity of everything pressing hard. "If I could get back to the river at the fortress in Toledo, maybe I could find a way home. Back to my time, and away from all of this danger."

Luca's eyes darken with sadness. "Is the danger gone in your time?" His voice is low. "What happens to my people?"

I swallow, knowing there's no easy way to say it. "The Crown will push even harder—complete Christianization, destroying entire villages, trying to erase centuries of culture and faith. The Inquisition will spread, hunting those who resist, branding them heretics. Families will continue to be torn apart."

His jaw tightens, and I see pain in his eyes. "More suffering."

I nod.

He looks at me. "If you try to go home, to your time, and you fail?"

"If I fail, I'll probably be caught again—or worse." I swallow hard. "I might be hanged by the guards, but I'm willing to risk that."

Luca's eyes search mine, heartbreak and worry swirling there.

"I have to try," I say. "To get back to my family, and to my time. I'm being hunted here, Luca. Back home, I have a safe and happy life."

He reaches out his hand, his eyes searching mine. "What about us? What about our love?"

The question breaks something inside me. I try to hold it back, but the tears come anyway, hot and sudden. I sob as everything crashes down on me—fear, loss, and impossible choices.

"I wish I could take you with me," I sputter between sobs. "I love you, Luca. I do. But I don't want to die here in 1492, not when I had a whole life back in 2025."

His hand tightens around mine. "I understand completely, Ava. And I'll do anything to get you back to the river safely. All I ask is for another day or two with you here, just a little time before I leave to set everything in motion. I'll prepare the safest way for you to get back to Toledo."

"Of course," I say, tears streaming down my cheeks. I throw my arms around him and add, "Thank you for saving me, believing me, and for forgiving me."

* * *

Luca and I slip away from the tiny village before the sun climbs too high, leaving Tomas and Matius to tend to their own errands in Toledo, checking on their families.

We wander into the orchards first, the sun pouring in through thick leaves heavy with ripening fruit. Luca plucks a ripe fig and offers it to me with a crooked smile. "For you, profesora."

I laugh, taking the fruit and biting into its sweetness. "You're quite the charmer."

We spend the morning chasing each other through meadows dotted with wildflowers, the tension of the past days slipping away with each shared glance and laugh. When Luca's hand brushes mine, I pretend that this moment isn't borrowed, and that time isn't a thief waiting to steal what we have.

The day rolls on, and we climb a gentle hill overlooking a breathtaking valley. We sit close, our shoulders touching, the quiet between us comfortable. I trace lazy patterns on his palm, feeling grounded by his touch.

As the sun dips low, we return to the garden behind Tomas's abuelo's home, where olive trees cast long shadows across the grass. A blanket is spread beneath the gnarled branches, worn but inviting.

A simple meal of bread, cheese, and olives awaits, laid out by Tomas's cousin Samira, who gives us a shy smile but wisely leaves us to our privacy.

We eat slowly, savoring more than just the food, enjoying each other's company. Luca leans in close, his voice low and teasing. "So, profesora, what's the lesson for today?"

I grin, brushing a stray lock of hair behind my ear. "That even in the darkest times, there can be light."

He nods and then brushes his lips across my knuckles.

I settle back on the blanket. "There's so much I want to tell you about the time I come from. Things you wouldn't believe."

Luca turns to me, his eyes bright with curiosity. "Tell me, then. What's so different about your time?"

I smile, trying to keep it light. "Well, for starters, there are these things called cars. They move faster than any horse, and you don't need to feed them or rest."

He blinks, clearly puzzled. "Carriages without horses? That sounds like magic."

I laugh. "Almost. And then there are phones—small devices that let you speak to someone far away, see their face, even send music or pictures."

Luca furrows his brow. "Pictures? What are those?"

I smile. "They're like drawings or paintings, but captured from real life in an instant. You can hold moments–people, places, events–frozen on a small glass screen. It's how we remember things and share them quickly."

He nods slowly, his eyes wide. "A magic window to the past and present all at once. Incredible."

I take a deep breath, feeling a little giddy sharing this with him. "There are also airplanes. Big metal birds that fly through the sky faster than anything you can imagine. People can ride in them and cross entire oceans in hours instead of weeks."

Luca's eyes fill with awe again. "Flying machines? That must be terrifying and wonderful."

"It is both," I admit with a smile. "And then there's something called movies. Stories told with moving pictures and sound, so everyone can watch and feel like they're part of the adventure."

He chuckles softly. "Stories that move and speak? Like enchanted plays?"

"Exactly," I say, warmth spreading in my chest. "It's like sitting by a fire sharing stories with friends, but the story comes alive on a screen."

Luca leans back on his elbows, gazing up at the stars beginning to twinkle above us. "Your world sounds… vast and strange. I wonder if you miss it terribly."

I nod. "I do. Sometimes it feels like a different life…but I wouldn't trade meeting you for anything."

For a few stolen hours, the world outside our blanket fades. No threats, no futures to fear, just two souls daring to love, if only for a little while.

The fading light casts a fragile glow through the tree branches, wrapping us in a deep twilight. Luca's hand finds mine again, his fingers tracing slow circles over my skin, sending shivers I can't hide.

He leans closer, his breath warm against my cheek. "You're so beautiful, Ava."

My heart races, and I close my eyes for a moment, savoring the way he makes me feel safe, wanted, like maybe this moment can hold us forever.

Without a word, his lips find mine. The kiss is passionate, urgent, powerful, and tender all at once, as if we're making up for lost time.

He moves his hands slowly, undoing the ties of my dress, revealing the curves of my breasts. His lips follow the path his fingers carve, pressing kisses along my collarbone and down to my shoulders. His tongue traces gentle, tantalizing patterns over every inch he uncovers, sending chills racing through my body.

Luca's lips explore with a hunger, mapping the familiar terrain of my skin as if discovering me anew. Each touch of his lips and finger-tips ignites sparks that pulse between us.

His hands pause at the edges of his own shirt, then with a swift motion, he pulls it over his head and lets it fall aside. The last traces of sunlight catch the lines of his chiseled chest and the strength in his muscular arms.

I push him over and roll onto him, the warmth of his skin pressing against mine. It's my turn now to explore the firm planes of his biceps, the rise and fall of his chest, the taut muscles of his abs. I trace every contour of the body that must've inspired Adonis, memorizing the strength and smoothness of Luca.

He catches my gaze and smiles, his voice low and rough. "You're amazing, Ava."

Encouraged, I slip my hands down to the waistband of his trousers, slowly undoing them. With a quiet shiver, I pull them off, revealing the hardness waiting for me. I settle down onto him, feeling the pulse of his desire inside of me as we move together, lost in the heat of the moment.

His hands roam over my breasts, hips, and the curve of my ass, steadying me as I ride him harder. Each touch fuels the fire building between us, urging us deeper into the rhythm we create together.

In his arms, I find a refuge from the chaos waiting beyond these trees, a place where love isn't borrowed or stolen, but fully ours.

Our movements grow faster, our breaths mingling and hearts pounding in unison. Every touch, every gasp, every whispered name pulls us closer to the edge.

Then, with a shuddering release, we climax together, waves of ecstasy crashing through us, grounding us in this moment of pure connection. I cling to him, feeling his heartbeat beneath my hand, knowing that whatever the future holds, this night is ours forever.

## 22

# SIXTY SOULS

## *LUCA*

WE RETURN to the small stone cottage where Samira and Tomas's abuelo live. Samira moves quietly, offering us blankets and fresh tea, but I barely notice. My thoughts churn like a storm beneath the calm surface.

Ava sits near the fire, her fingers wrapped tightly around her cup. She looks tired, but there's a strange light in her eyes, a mix of hope and fear that mirrors the turmoil inside me. The truth she shared today, that she is from another time, a future I can't fathom, hangs between us, thick and unspoken now.

I want to believe her, and part of me does. She spoke with such conviction, such certainty. She knows things about the world and history that no one here could possibly know. The name Cristóbal Colón slipped from her lips with a gravity I can't ignore. And that message about the bathhouses–it was from her, sent to help us. How could she have known its whereabouts? How could she have cracked and invented codes so easily?

But it's hard to reconcile that part of her with the woman I have come to care for deeply. How do I hold on to someone who says she doesn't belong here, who says she's already lived another life, one far away from me and this place? The thought twists my gut.

I lie awake long after Ava falls into a restless sleep, my eyes fixed on the shadows dancing across the ceiling. I imagine the future she spoke of, the world beyond these forests and stone walls, where our king and queen are long forgotten and where time moves differently. Is that where she truly belongs? And if so, what am I to her?

The thought of losing her feels like a physical ache, like ice pressing against my skin. I want to fight for her, to hold her here, but I know she's made her choice. She wants to go home, back to her family and the life she once knew, and I can't blame her.

Still, I wonder whether, if I could, if I would find a way to follow her, to step into that strange future and meet the world she describes. Or would I be lost there, a stranger without roots?

The unspoken words between us press down harder than the darkness around me. I want to ask her more, to understand everything she means, but the fear of shattering this fragile trust holds me back.

Instead, I reach out, letting my fingers brush hers gently in the quiet night. She moves a little, but doesn't awaken. I trace the curve of her hand, memorizing the feel, knowing that this might be one of the last times I can touch her.

Tomorrow, everything changes. She will try to find her way back to the Tagus, to whatever chance remains for her to escape this time and all the horrors she says will come. I'm terrified, not just for her, but for myself, because losing her means losing a part of me I never expected to find.

I close my eyes and hold on to the moment as tightly as I can. Love isn't always about holding on, but knowing when to let go.

* * *

I awaken to the soft rustle of Ava and Samira cooking breakfast.

While we eat, I explain my plans to Ava. "I'm going back to Toledo tonight. I'll ride under the cover of darkness. I have to help Abuela Maria and as many others escape as possible. If what you say is true...

134

if more danger is coming, then I need to get them out. Slowly, in small groups, before anyone notices."

Ava swallows hard, nodding, but I see the fear in her eyes. I feel it too. The stakes have never been higher.

"It won't be easy," I add quickly. "But it's the best chance they have."

Her hand finds mine, squeezing gently. "You're so brave, Luca." She pulls me closer, resting her head against my shoulder.

"We have one more day," I say softly, tracing circles on her back. "One more day to forget everything else. To just be together."

"One more day," she says with a sigh.

We spend the morning wrapped in that quiet understanding. Samira leaves us space, knowing this day belongs to us.

As the sun sets, we sit beneath the olive trees, sharing a simple meal on the worn blanket. Our conversation drifts between whispered dreams and stolen laughter, but always shadowed by the darkness of what's coming.

Night deepens, and I hold Ava close beneath the stars, willing the moment to stretch, to hold us safe just a little longer.

Tonight, I leave for Toledo, and everything will change, but right now, there is only the two of us.

* * *

THE MOON SLIPS BEHIND A VEIL OF CLOUDS AS I STAND AT THE EDGE OF the village, my breath shallow, my heart pounding like a drum. Ava's hand trembles in mine, warm and fragile, like she might disappear if I let go.

"I have to leave now," I whisper, my voice tight with everything I'm holding back.

Her eyes are glossy. "Promise me you'll come back," she says, her voice breaking, the words barely more than a breath.

"I swear it," I say, pulling her close, feeling the heat of her skin against mine.

Our lips meet, hesitant at first, then hungry and fierce, like we're trying to cram a lifetime into one kiss. My hands cradle her face, memorizing every curve, every line. I silently plea to the heavens for more time.

Tears slip down her cheeks, and I catch them on my thumbs, swallowing the lump in my throat.

"I don't want to lose you," she says, her voice raw.

"You won't," I promise. "I'm coming back. No matter what."

She clings to me, her arms tight around my neck, as if I'm the only thing holding her to this world.

"I love you, Ava."

"I love you, too, Luca."

I hold her for one last moment then reluctantly step back, my fingers brushing hers before I turn and disappear into the dark woods.

Every step away from her feels like tearing my soul in two. But I'll be back. I have to be.

The road back to Toledo is rough but familiar, and I push through the darkened streets with purpose. Every step brings me closer to the heart of the city, and to the plan I must put into motion.

I slip through a quiet alley and reach Abuela Maria's house. She's waiting, as if she sensed I'd come. Her tired eyes brighten with cautious hope when she sees me.

"Luca," she says softly, pulling me inside.

"There's little time," I begin without hesitation. "The holy officers are tightening their grip. We need to move as many people as we can out of sight."

She nods solemnly, knowing what's coming.

"The bathhouse," I say, "it's large—more than I realized. Hidden beneath the city, it's perfect for shelter. I plan to bring in as many of our people as I can. Families, friends, anyone at risk."

Her face tightens. "But can we keep them safe there?"

"We will," I say firmly. "We'll guard the entrances, keep watch over every corner. No one will enter or leave without my word."

She exhales slowly, her hands finding mine. "This is a heavy burden."

"It's necessary," I reply. "Once they're hidden, I'll arrange to move small groups out quietly, far from the city, when the time is right."

*  *  *

THE PLAN IS SET. NOW, ALL THAT REMAINS IS TO BRING EVERYONE safely inside the bathhouse, and wait for the moment we can lead them to freedom.

The moment I leave Abuela Maria's house, the magnitude of what lies ahead settles deep in my chest. Every step back through Toledo is measured, careful, but my mind races faster than my feet can carry me.

I find a quiet corner near the market where I can send the messages, Ava's code–the patterns, the symbols, the hidden signals woven into seemingly innocent drawings and letters. It's the only way to speak without alerting the holy officers. I work quickly, etching the code onto scraps of parchment and slipping them into the hands of trusted allies: Tomas, Matius, Catalina, and many others who have pledged their loyalty.

The message is simple, yet urgent. *Meet at the bathhouse after dusk. Bring weapons, supplies, travel light.*

Word spreads like wildfire through the underground channels. I watch faces brighten with hope, hear hushed conversations filled with relief.

Night falls, and one by one, they arrive. Families clutching what little they can carry. Mothers carrying children. Old men limping on worn canes. Young men and women with fierce determination burning in their gaze.

I guide them inside, moving swiftly but with care. The bathhouse is cavernous, more immense than anyone suspected, with winding tunnels and chambers beneath the city. The stone walls echo faintly with the sound of dripping water and hurried footsteps.

"This way," I say, leading a group through a narrow corridor that opens into a large vaulted chamber. Flickering lanterns cast shadows over ancient, empty mikvahs.

I count heads carefully. Nearly sixty souls so far, and more trickle in from side passages.

Once everyone is inside and accounted for, we will wait. When the time is right, I will organize small groups to slip out under cover of darkness, finding refuge in villages beyond the city's reach.

I look around the chamber, at the faces lit by lantern glow—hope, fear, trust, all tangled together. This is more than shelter. This is survival.

I think of Ava. Her courage and vision. Without her, this plan would never have come together.

I stand in the center of the chamber, the air thick with the mingled scent of damp stone and sweat, and let my gaze sweep over the sixty lives now depending on me. The bathhouse hums quietly with whispers and the rustle of blankets, a fragile bubble of safety in a city ready to crush us.

Somewhere out there, Ava is moving toward her own uncertain fate, just as I am toward mine. I can almost hear her voice in the silence, urging me to keep going, to not falter. I grip the hilt of my dagger, not for the fight I know is coming, but as a promise to her, to Abuela Maria, to everyone huddled in these shadows, that I will see this through. One step, one night, one escape at a time until they are free.

Until I can return to her.

2 3

---

# LOVE AND DEATH

*AVA*

THE DAYS slip past in a blur of work and worry. Samira and her abuelo's home sits on the edge of a small valley, its whitewashed walls and low clay roof sheltered by olive and orange trees.

I wake each morning to the smell of baking bread, the sound of roosters, and to the creak of the wooden shutters swinging open as Samira lets sunlight into the little house.

I try not to think about where Luca is or whether he's in danger, but every other moment, every pause between chores, my mind rushes back to him.

In the mornings, we tend to her abuelo, who lies in a large bed in the back room. His raspy breath comes slowly, but his eyes still brighten when Samira speaks to him. She feeds him broth, adjusts the blankets, smooths the creases in his brow. I help when I can, fetching water from the well, holding the cup to his lips when her hands are full.

Samira smiles when I help, but it's the kind of smile that knows how heavy life can be. She's stunningly beautiful, a beauty that would turn heads anywhere, yet there's no mistaking the sorrow hiding in her eyes. It's a quiet proof that she's been through hell and come out the other side.

After breakfast, we go to the orchard. The air is sharp with the smell of citrus. Lemon trees bend with their fruit, and oranges glow like suns in the green foliage. Samira shows me how to twist the fruit just so, so the stem gives way without tearing the branch. We fill baskets until our arms ache.

"Here," she says, handing me a fig. "Best eaten right from the tree."

It's warm from the sun and sweet. For a second, I almost forget the year, the hunt, the gnawing ache in my chest, but thoughts of Luca are never far.

That night, lying in bed, I picture his dark eyes, the way his hand brushes mine like it's the most natural thing in the world. I think about the last time I saw him, and how every minute since feels like walking on a tightrope with no net.

By the fourth day, Samira watches me more closely.

"You work hard," she says that afternoon in the garden, her hands buried in the soil as she plants seedlings. "But sometimes I see you stop. Your eyes go far away, like you've left your body."

I press my hands into the dirt, trying to anchor myself. "Do I?"

She nods. "You miss him."

I pause. The truth is so much more than that, but I also know she thinks she's being kind, giving me an easy explanation.

"Of course I miss Luca," I say. My voice catches, and I have to look down at the row of green shoots before me. "But it's not just that."

Samira sits back on her heels, wiping her hands on her skirt. "If you're worried about the guards, they'll never find you here."

I take a breath, the air heavy with rosemary and thyme from the herb bed. "It's not just the guards or being in hiding either. I'm trying to make an impossible decision. Love or safety. Love and death… or a loveless life."

Her brows lift, surprise pouring over her face at the tangle of my problems. She stays quiet, the pause stretching long enough for me to wonder if I've said too much.

Finally, she leans forward again, planting another sprout. "That is a difficult choice," she says softly. "But in this world, there will only ever be one Luca."

Her words settle over me. Somehow, across time and centuries, I was meant to find him, to love him. I wasn't sent here only to save people. I was sent to find Luca, the one I'm meant to hold, to cherish, to build a life with.

How can I just walk away from him? How can I return to a future where he's nothing more than a name in a dusty history book, a man who died in a forgotten rebellion brawl, long before I could reach him?

The thought twists my heart into knots. Love and time... braided in ways I don't know how to unravel.

The problem is my world doesn't fade away. It keeps intruding. The year 2025 is still out there, waiting for me, pulling me back toward my family and security. But security there means no Luca. Staying here means I could lose everything, including my life.

That night, after Samira has gone to bed, I sit on the blanket in the garden, looking up at a sky so crowded with stars it almost hurts to stare. The air is cool, with the scent of orange blossoms drifting from the orchard.

I try to imagine a life where I choose to go back home to the future, but where my heart never quite forgets what it gave up. Then I try to picture choosing Luca with his warmth and laughter, but always with the shadow of danger at our heels.

By the end of the week, I'm more tired than when I arrived. The work doesn't exhaust me. The constant turning over of options in my head does. I think Samira can see it.

On the seventh evening, we carry baskets of herbs into the kitchen. She sings as she hangs bunches of rosemary from the rafters. I catch my reflection in the small metal mirror on the wall near the table. My face looks puffy. My eyes have dark circles under them.

Samira glances at me but says nothing. I think she knows I wouldn't be able to answer even if she asked.

When I finally crawl into bed, the words she said in the garden circle through my mind.

*There will only ever be one Luca.*

She's right. This choice is between the love of my life and the rest of my life.

I thought I was certain I wanted to go back home to my family where I could live a long and fulfilled, happy life, but every time I close my eyes and see Luca's face, my love for him is so strong, it hurts.

## 24

# BACK TO THE TAGUS

## *LUCA*

THE WEEK HAS PASSED by quickly in rushed footsteps, whispered plans, and tired faces. One by one, I've guided families out of the bathhouse's dark sanctuary, through winding paths, and far beyond Toledo's grasp.

Each family I send away carries a fragment of hope that the holy officers won't find them, that their children will grow free beneath a sky untouched by fear.

I tell them firmly, again and again, "Keep moving. Don't stay too close. The Crown's oppression will spread like wildfire, faster than any man can outrun."

At the edge of a quiet village where the road forks into the hills, I watch the last group disappear into the trees, shadows swallowing their shapes. My heart clenches, knowing I may never see some of them again, but their safety must come first.

The journey back to the village where Ava waits feels heavier than the days spent leading the families out. The road twists beneath my boots, but my mind races ahead to her... to the way her eyes hold so much passion and spirit, and the way her hand fits perfectly in mine. I ache to see her, to hold her, even as the weight of what lies ahead for us presses down.

When I reach the small cottage, the fading light paints her silhouette against the trees. She looks up as I step onto the path, and a fragile smile breaks across her face, beautiful and bright, even if I know it hides so much pain.

"Ava," I say, my voice rough from dust and days without rest.

She crosses the yard in a few quick strides, and we meet halfway, the world shrinking to just us. I pull her close, feeling the warmth of her body.

"We did it," I say. "They're safe for now."

Her breath catches, and I trace the line of her jaw. "Luca, *you* did it! You saved so many people! Did you tell them to put as much distance between themselves and this country as they could?"

"Yes. I told them the danger isn't over. The Crown will hunt them relentlessly."

She nods, her eyes dark with unshed tears. "And us?"

I swallow the lump rising in my throat. "You and I... we have time, but it's borrowed. I can't stop thinking about how much I want to hold you forever, and how every moment is a gift stolen from the future that pulls you back."

Her fingers tighten around mine. "I'm scared."

"So am I," I admit.

We step inside the small cottage. Samira is there, her eyes full of curiosity and concern. She sets down a basket and moves closer.

"How did it go?" she asks.

I drop my pack by the door and run a hand through my hair, exhaustion threading every movement. "It was harder than I imagined." I take a deep breath. "Sixty people, maybe more."

Ava's fingers find mine, giving a small squeeze.

"The bathhouse was huge. It gave them shelter, but it was cramped and tense. We moved in small groups under cover of darkness, slipping through the shadows."

Samira listens intently, nodding as I speak.

"But the worst part," I say, my voice low, "was knowing the holy officers will never cease. They're spreading terror across the city.

Even the villages and towns. If we stay close to Toledo, they'll find us, eventually."

"You both carry burdens heavier than these walls, but you're not alone," Samira says.

Samira and Ava move quietly around the small room, their gentle presence a comfort to my worn body. Samira brings a simple plate of bread and fruit, while Ava kneels beside me, easing my boots off. The ache in my feet starts to fade as she massages my ankles, then hands me a cup of cool water and a glass of wine.

When they help me into bed, the soft mattress welcomes me like a long-lost friend. I close my eyes, and finally, I let sleep claim me.

* * *

The morning light pours through the windows as I find Ava sitting at the edge of the bed, her hands in her lap, her eyes puffy and red.

"We need to get you back to the Tagus," I say gently.

She nods but doesn't speak. After a long pause, tears spill down her cheeks. I reach for her face, tilting it up to meet my lips with hers. She leans into me, wraps her arms around my waist, and pulls me closer.

"I don't want to leave. I want to stay with you."

I cup her face, my thumb tracing the line of her jaw. "I want you here, more than anything." I brush my lips along her cheek, then her temple, savoring every inch. "But it's not safe for you. The future is where you belong. It's where you're protected."

She presses her forehead to mine, trembling. "How can the universe ask me to choose between love and safety?"

"Ava, I love you enough to let you go." My voice cracks, but I hold her steady. I kiss her again, slow, lingering, like trying to memorize the taste of her lips. "Part of loving you is protecting you, even if it means standing aside."

"I'm afraid I'll never see you again."

"Then I'll find my way back to you," I vow, holding her close. "We have one more day. One more night. I'll fill every moment with kisses and whispers, with all the love I have."

I trail my hands down her back, memorizing the curve of her waist, the warmth of her skin beneath my fingers. Outside, the orchard basks in sunlight, but inside, time slows until it feels like only we exist.

At twilight, beneath a blanket of stars, I pull her close again. My lips find hers, soft, urgent, each kiss a promise and a prayer. Her hands slide beneath my shirt. We cling to each other like the world might crumble if we let go.

Later, by the firelight's glow, we sit together hand in hand. "Tonight," I murmur, "I'll take you to the river by the castle, just before dawn. That's when you first came through."

The fire sputters low in the kitchen as we pack the last of our things. Outside, the village sleeps under a sky heavy with stars.

Ava steps toward Samira. "Thank you, Samira. For everything. For shelter, kindness, and for your friendship."

Samira smiles. "You're part of this family now. You always will be."

I step beside Ava, resting a hand lightly on her back. "We'll leave now. The path to Toledo is long, and we must be cautious."

Ava squeezes Samira's hand, and I catch the tremor in her fingers. I know this goodbye presses hard on her heart.

The night is still as we saddle the horses. I help Ava up, my fingers lingering on her waist a moment longer than necessary. Her eyes search mine, and I feel that fierce mix of love and fear that has become our constant companion.

We ride through the sleeping village, the sound of hooves on the earth, and reach the outskirts of Toledo just as the horizon blurs between night and day. The old stone walls of the palace rise like ghosts in the morning mist, and ahead, the Tagus gleams faintly, churning and deep.

I pull the reins, guiding the horses to a quiet spot beneath a gnarled tree overlooking the water. The world feels impossibly still. We dismount and tie the horses to the tree.

Ava turns to me, her eyes shimmering with unshed tears. "This is where I came through the first time."

I cup her face, brushing a stray lock of hair behind her ear. "And this is where I'll hold you until you're safe again. No matter what happens next."

As we kiss, the rush of water, the cool morning breeze, all fade away, leaving only the two of us, suspended in time's fragility.

The sun peeks over the horizon, shimmering gold across the water's surface, and this moment feels like the end of everything.

"I love you, Ava," I whisper.

Her smile is small but brave. "I love you."

Together, we stand next to the river, waiting for the dawn to fully break, and for the impossible door to open once more.

## 25

---

# ALCAZAR DE TOLEDO

### *AVA*

DAWN SOFTENS THE SKY, painting the outer walls of the Castillo de San Servando in pale pink and gold. Luca holds me close, his breath warm on my neck. My heart beats wildly against his chest as our faces draw nearer, the promise of a last kiss hanging between us.

Then, without warning, the quiet shatters.

"Seize them!" a harsh voice orders.

Three guards emerge suddenly from the shadows, swift and ruthless. Panic explodes inside me. I try to pull back, but Luca's grip tightens, protective and fierce.

The first guard lunges at me, his fingers like blades cutting into my arm. I struggle, but two hands yank me away from Luca, tearing me out of his embrace as another guard draws his knife and lurches toward us.

"Luca!" I shout, desperation cracking my voice.

Luca draws his dagger and spins toward the third guard, who charges at him. The glint of steel catches the light as Luca plunges his blade deep. The guard collapses with a choking sound, but two others hold me, dragging me backward.

My feet scrape against the edge of the shore, the Tagus River below, dark and unforgiving.

"Hold her tight," one guard snarls, and my arms are wrenched behind me. I bite back a cry as the world narrows to the sharp grip on my wrists.

Luca's eyes meet mine for a moment, desperate, and then I'm pulled further from him. There are two of them, and one stands tall, sword in hand, between us as the other pulls me away.

The dawn light catches the glint of Luca's dagger once more as he prepares for the fight ahead, but I'm already slipping away, caught in rough hands that don't care if I scream.

Before I can catch my breath, I'm shoved into a creaking wooden wagon waiting just across the bridge. The smell of hay and dust fills the cramped space as the guards slam the wagon door shut. I press my face to the splintered wood.

"Where are you taking me?" I ask, my voice hoarse.

The nearest guard sneers. "The dungeon under the castle," he says over his shoulder.

"But the castle's back there by the river."

"Not that one," another guard grunts. "We're going to Alcázar. That's where they keep prisoners like you."

The wagon jolts forward, and the sound of wheels crunching over pebbles fades behind me. My mind races, trying to piece together what horrors await beneath the walls of the fortress, a place far from the Tagus River's flowing waters where I'd hoped for escape.

Darkness closes in around me again, but this time it's not just the absence of light. It's the heavy weight of uncertainty, of a fate sealed somewhere deep within the dungeon of the Alcázar.

They thrust me into a cell, the heavy iron door slamming shut with a finality that turns my stomach. The room is smaller than I expected, but it feels endless in the darkness. No windows, only the faintest crack at the top letting in a thin sliver of morning light.

My hands tremble as I try to control my breath. The rough walls trap me in a silence so deep it hums in my ears. I press my back against the cold, damp wall, the weight of everything crashing down.

Where is Luca? Did he get away? Is he hurt? The thought of losing him stabs into my gut like a knife. I close my eyes, trying to will him to find me, but all I feel is emptiness.

Voices outside my cell echo faintly, a mixture of low murmurs and clipped orders. I catch a fragment of a sentence—"heretic," "aiding enemies," "council must decide." My blood runs cold.

I know exactly what councils and trials decide in this era. I've studied the Inquisition's courts closely. They conduct merciless interrogations and twist every word until there is no hope left. They break even the strongest of people. I want to scream, to cry, to fight, but the darkness swallows everything.

I'm trapped.

If only I could get to the river. If only I could dive into the water and disappear beneath the surface, and escape this nightmare.

But I've been caught—again—and for now, all I have are these cold walls, and the steady rising of my own panic.

A distant clang startles me–chains, footsteps, doors opening and closing. The guards are still here.

I press my palms against the wall, searching for any weakness, any crack, anything that might lead me out. I desperately trace my fingers over the rough stone. The dawn outside grows brighter, but here, beneath the castle, time feels frozen.

* * *

ROUGH HANDS SEIZE ME, YANKING ME UPRIGHT. THE COLD DAMPNESS of the dungeon clings to my skin, but a deeper chill spreads through me when I hear a gruff voice.

"You're to come with us," a guard growls, gripping my arm. "The queen wants to see the blue-eyed rebel woman."

Fear crashes over me in waves. Blue-eyed rebel woman? The last thing I need is to anger Queen Isabella.

They drag me from the dark cell and up the winding steps. Torchlight flickers along the ancient walls, casting dancing shadows. Above, towering battlements stretch toward the high ceiling, their cold granite softened only by intricate tapestries depicting battles and kings long dead. The scent of aged leather and smoke lingers in the air, mingling with the faint metallic tang of old armor displayed in polished racks.

Massive oak doors studded with iron rivets open into a great hall, where echoes bounce off vaulted ceilings supported by thick columns carved with heraldic symbols. Stained glass windows filter the sunlight into jewel-toned patterns across the flagstone floor.

I'm shoved through the grand doorway into a vast chamber filled with silence and cold, sharp eyes. Queen Isabella sits on her throne, unmoving, her gaze fixed on me without a word.

The courtiers behind her watch silently, their faces masks of curiosity and disdain.

I drop to my knees, trembling, my mind racing with terror. This must be the moment they decide my fate, the moment I lose everything.

The queen's gaze fixes on me, sharp and unyielding. Without a word, she rises from her throne, the rustle of her silk gown echoing through the chamber. Step by deliberate step, she approaches, her presence filling the vast room like a storm barely contained.

When she stops just inches from me, the air between us thickens. Her sapphire eyes bore into me, piercing, almost hypnotic. There's a cold beauty in her, and an undeniable power that commands obedience.

She leans in, close enough that I can feel her breath, cool and scented faintly of mint and smoke. The tiniest curl of a smile, almost mocking, touches her lips. It's both terrifying and mesmerizing.

After what feels like an eternity, Queen Isabella straightens, and her eyes trace briefly over the room. She mutters to no one in particular, her voice sharp and cold, "Her eyes are nowhere near as blue as mine."

Without another word, the queen dismisses the gathering with the flick of her wrist, turning her attention away and sending me back to the darkness.

Back in the pitch-black cell, I press my back to the wall, closing my eyes, wishing for the comfort of Luca's strong arms.

The shadows curl around me like a suffocating cloak. Outside, faint footsteps echo, too far away to be a rescue. The thick air tastes of mildew. My mind races, grasping for anything that might be a way out.

I try to piece together what I know of this castle's layout. The staircases must twist and turn above these walls. Somewhere there must be a forgotten passage, a loose stone, a rusted grate, anything. I press my fingers into the mortar between the masonry, feeling for a crack, a weakness. But it's solid, unyielding.

The cold seeps into my bones as I sink to the floor, curling my arms around my knees. This castle was built long ago, a maze designed not just to keep invaders out, but prisoners in. Dungeons like this were made to break people's spirits, to make them give up hope.

I listen for the rhythm of footsteps again, and for voices. The *trial,* that dreaded word, circles my mind, tightening like a noose. I know the Inquisition shows no mercy. Accusations mean torture, confessions forced by pain, and no chance to plead my cause.

Time stretches. My muscles ache from sitting on the hard floor for too long, but I force myself to stay alert. If I'm to escape, it will have to be before dawn gives way to the full light of day.

A faint scraping sound at the door startles me. A small slot opens, and a piece of moldy bread and a chipped wooden bowl of water are slid inside.

A rough voice mutters, "Your trial is tomorrow, at the noon hour."

The door clanks shut before I can ask a question. I stare at the meager food, tasting nothing but bitter fear.

# 26

## HIS NAME IS LUCA

### *AVA*

THE CLANGING of iron wakes me. My eyes snap open to thick blackness, and the damp air that clings to my skin like a cold, heavy shroud. The scent of mildew curls in the corners of the cell. My body aches from the hard floor beneath me, every bone and muscle stiff and sore.

Somewhere in the depths of the night, exhaustion dragged me under, but now, waking, I don't know how long I've slept.

I lie still for a moment, straining to catch my breath. Somewhere far beyond these walls, I imagine the Tagus River flowing, and clutch that thought tightly. I may still have a chance to get back home.

The scrape of a key in the lock shatters the silence. The heavy door groans open.

"Up." The bark of a guard's voice bounces off the walls.

Hands seize my arms and haul me upright before I can find my footing. My legs protest, trembling with stiffness and cold, but I'm forced to move. The guards grip me tightly, dragging me forward through hallways, where the damp stone gives way to a warmth that smells faintly of citrus and lavender.

We emerge into a long corridor lined with towering pillars. At the far end, a council of robed men sits. Their faces are as still as masks.

Their eyes track me, cold as ice, as the guards shove me forward. The sound of my boots scraping the floor is too loud in the vaulted chamber. I force myself to keep my chin lifted, though my stomach tightens with sour dread.

One of the men rises, his voice low and merciless. "Woman–" He pauses, as if realizing none of them even bothered with my name, that to them, I'm nothing more than a criminal and a woman, which is often worse. "You stand accused of sedition, heresy, and treachery against the Crown."

The words hang in the air, final and unyielding, like a noose tightening around my throat.

Another leans forward. "The council has deliberated. Your sentence is death. You will meet your end at dawn tomorrow."

*Dawn. Less than a day away.*

They don't specify the manner of my death yet, only the certainty that it will come at dawn.

"Have you anything to say for yourself?" The question is sharp, a blade waiting to cut.

For a split second, my mind goes blank. Then, quietly, I find my voice. "If I may... I wish to confess my sins before my death. Please, allow me to speak to a priest."

A murmur ripples through the council like dry leaves stirred by a cold wind. The presiding man inclines his head slightly. "One will be sent to your cell."

The guards seize my arms again, hauling me roughly back the way we came.

The dungeon swallows me again. Heavy door slams shut with a finality that churns my stomach. The lock clicks.

I sink to the floor, my knees drawn tight against my chest, the chill of death pressing in from every side. Tomorrow at dawn... I have hours to make peace, or find a way out.

Time stretches unbearably in the thick darkness. My thoughts circle endlessly, restless as trapped animals. I rub my wrists where the shackles bit into my skin, flex my stiff fingers, and pace the short length of the cell.

Someone puts a key in the lock again. Expecting more guards, or another command I must obey, I brace myself, but instead, a single figure steps into the cell, holding a single candle.

The priest is older, his back bowed. His plain brown robes fall in gentle folds, his hair silver at the temples. His face is kind but deeply lined, as if each sorrow he's heard has etched itself into his skin.

"You requested confession, my child," he says softly, his voice a comfort in the darkness.

I nod, throat tight. "Yes, Father."

I say a silent prayer that the guards do not follow him inside. The door thuds closed behind him, sealing us in the chill silence.

He kneels on the cold stone floor opposite me and sets the candle next to him. "Then speak, my child."

I inhale deeply, searching for the right words. "I will, but first, I need your help more than confession. I have someone outside these walls who needs to know what has happened to me."

His brow furrows, the weight of his years and duties pressing in. "Why? What have you done that demands such secrecy?"

"I have done no harm," I say quickly, my voice slightly louder than I intend. "All I did was help people escape the city. We helped families, children, those who would have been killed if they had stayed. They call it treason, but it was mercy. I did nothing but try to save lives."

My throat tightens as I add, "I am not a criminal, Father. If I am left here with no one to speak for me, their lies will become the only story told."

He studies my face, searching for truth in my eyes.

I lean forward, urgency sharpening my words. "Please, I beg you. I have no family here. No advocate. But there is one who would risk everything to help me. He must know before dawn."

The priest frowns. "You wish for me to carry a message?"

"Yes. I beg you."

The lines around his mouth soften just slightly, a glimmer of understanding in his eyes. "This is dangerous," he murmurs.

"I know." I fold my hands as if in prayer. "But they won't search a priest, and they won't suspect a confession."

His gaze falls briefly to the floor, then returns, gentler now. "If I do this, the message must be meaningless to others."

Hope sparks deep inside me. "It will be. I'll write it in a code only he and I understand."

After a pause, he reaches into his pocket and produces a thin sheet of parchment and a stub of charcoal. "You must write quickly."

The rough texture of the parchment feels like a lifeline. I kneel and use the floor as a surface to draw shapes and lines on the paper that only Luca can read.

When I finish, I fold the paper carefully and press it into the priest's palm. Our eyes meet, heavy with urgency. "Promise me, Father. Promise you will get this to him tonight. His name is Luca. He will be leading a meeting at the bathhouse in the Jewish quarter, east of the city." I hesitate, then add, "It might not be easy for you to reach him. You must make sure they know you come in peace. Tell them you are a priest sent to deliver a message. Please, I beg you, this letter must reach him as soon as possible."

He sighs and shakes his head slowly. "This is a dangerous task, far more dangerous than simply leaving this place with this message. If I'm caught with this in the streets—"

"I understand and greatly appreciate the risk," I say quietly, cutting him off. "But I believe you follow your faith because it teaches mercy. I'm no criminal. I only helped people escape the city to keep them safe. Now, I need help myself."

He studies me for a moment. Finally, he nods. "Very well. I'll do what I can."

"Thank you, Father," I whisper. "May God keep you safe."

He closes his fingers over the note, tucks it into his pocket, and nods solemnly.

The lock turns again, and the guards return. As they lead the priest away, I clutch the thought that somewhere beyond these walls, Luca will read my words long before the dawn breaks.

# 27

# THANK YOU, PADRE

## *LUCA*

THE COLUMNS RISE LIKE SENTRIES, their carvings worn smooth by centuries. The abandoned bathhouse has been my post since yesterday morning, and it will stay that way until I hear from Ava.

It keeps replaying in my head. I see her in the pale light of dawn, close enough for me to feel the warmth of her breath, her fingers curled tight around mine. We were leaning in, ready to steal a goodbye kiss, when the sound of boots hit stone.

The guards were on her in seconds. I went for the officer who stood between us first, my dagger in my fist. It sank between his ribs before he even knew I'd struck. Still, the other two dragged her to the wagon, her cries lost in the rattle of its wheels.

I followed as far as I could, across the bridge, through the market, but the moment they reached the castle gates, I knew where they took her. Beneath the castle... and in those black cells, hope doesn't last long.

Since then, Tomas, Matius, Martin, Luis, and I have been working every angle we can think of. Bribes, favors, and half-baked plans. Every path ends the same way: too many guards, too little time.

So I wait here. If she gets a chance to send word, she'll send it here. She knows this place, knows it's ours, and she's clever enough to get a message out, even from there. But the dungeon isn't just trouble. It's life or death.

A shard of clay skitters across the floor, and I snap my head up. Footsteps approach, quick and uneven. Tomas appears from the shadows, breathing hard. The look on his face makes my stomach drop before he even speaks.

"What is it?" My voice echoes low in the empty chamber.

He glances back toward the stairwell, making sure we're alone. "News from the castle."

I'm already moving toward him. "Tell me."

He hesitates, his jaw tight. "They brought her to trial at noon."

The words hit like a punch, but I force myself to stay still. "And? What is her punishment?"

Tomas swallows. "She was sentenced to death."

The silence in the bathhouse grows heavier, pressing in from every side. Somewhere behind me, Martin mutters a curse under his breath. Luis looks away, as if not seeing me will make it untrue.

*Life or death.*

It's certain death now unless I find a way to get her back.

I don't care who sees me. The strength I've been holding onto tightly, like a rope burning in my hands, finally snaps. My knees hit the cracked tile. My chest folds in on itself, and the first sound that escapes me doesn't even feel like my own voice. It's raw and ugly.

I press my palms to my face, but it doesn't stop the shaking. Doesn't stop the heat burning behind my eyes.

I've been stoic throughout all of it. Through losing my family. Through watching friends bleed out in the street while the guards laughed. Through sending the last of my people, my friends, out of the city. Abuela Maria, half the men I trusted, women and children who couldn't hide from the holy officers forever. I told them to go, promised I'd be fine, promised I'd keep fighting.

But this... Ava....

Ava, who risked everything for people she didn't even know. They're going to kill her for standing between their cruelty and the helpless.

I push past Tomas without a word, my boots striking hard on the tile as I head for the farthest end of the bathhouse. The shadows darken there, where the columns give way to an arched tunnel leading deeper underground. I don't need to light a torch. I know the way.

The air grows colder the further I go, the walls narrowing until they're close enough to brush my shoulders. I find the small hollow, a dead-end chamber carved from the rock centuries ago. It's quiet enough here to allow myself to grieve.

I sink to the ground, back against the wall, and let it all out. The weight of every loss I've shoved down crashes through me at once.

I remember the way she looked yesterday morning, her hair catching the light, her lips just about to meet mine before they ripped her away. I remember the sound of her voice, and the way her beautiful eyes danced when she laughed.

I remember every moment, even the ones where I told myself we'd have more time.

If I stay here too long, I know I'll break in a way I can't fix, but I can't move yet. Not until the ache in my chest dulls enough for me to breathe without feeling like I'm drowning.

For the first time in years, I don't feel like the man who can fix everything. I feel like a man who's about to lose the only thing left that matters.

I don't know how long I sit there in the dark, my thoughts circling —the touch of her hand, her scent, the fact that in days, maybe hours, she'll be gone.

Footsteps echo down the tunnel. At first, I think it's just the sound of the city above bleeding through the stone, but then a silhouette breaks the darkness.

"Luca," Tomas's voice carries, low but urgent.

I drag my sleeve across my face and push myself up, but it feels like I'm moving underwater. "What is it?"

"There's someone here to see you."

The words don't make sense at first. Who would come here? No one outside our circle knows this place.

I follow him back through the narrow tunnel, the light from the main chamber stinging my eyes after so long in the dark. I try to guess: one of the allies we'd thought was gone? Someone with news of a way into the castle?

When I step into the open space, I stop cold. It's a priest wearing brown robes, a plain wooden cross hanging from his neck, his hands folded before him.

For a moment, my mind only registers the danger. A priest here, in the midst of all this, where priests serve the holy officers, where faith is a weapon they wield against people like us, feels like an enemy walking straight into our camp.

He doesn't speak right away. Instead, he steps forward and offers a folded scrap of parchment. "This is from the woman taken yesterday morning."

I snatch it from his hand before I can stop myself, my eyes scanning the familiar strokes of her handwriting. The message is short, but it's in the code only we know. It's from her, and she's alive.

"Thank you," I manage, my voice rough. "Thank you, Padre."

He nods once, calm as if we're meeting in daylight on a quiet street instead of here, where one wrong move could get us both killed.

Before he turns to go, I stop him. "Why?" The word comes out sharper than I intend, and I soften it. "Why risk everything for a woman you don't even know?"

The priest studies me for a moment, his gaze steady. "I could see she has a good heart, and the world needs more good hearts." He touches the cross on his chest. "I'll be praying for you both."

For a man I thought might be an enemy, his words hit somewhere deep. I clear my throat. "Then I thank you again, Padre. Truly."

He nods and then slips away, his steps fading toward the street above.

I stand there, the parchment clutched in my hand, my pulse still pounding. Ava's alive, and she's reaching out for me.

I read it twice, three times, tracing the familiar loops and slashes of her coded words until I'm sure I've got it right.

The fog I've been living in since yesterday burns away. My chest still aches, but it's no longer crushing the life out of me.

Tomas waits nearby, watching me with that sharp, restless look of his. "Well?"

"She's still breathing," I say, tucking the parchment into my pocket. "And she's not giving up."

That's all he needs to hear. He exchanges a glance with Matius, who's been leaning against a column, his arms folded. "We'll start immediately," Matius says quietly.

I explain the plan to all four of my best men, and Martin and Luis are already muttering to each other in the corner, sorting through whatever supplies we'll need.

Tomas and Matius will slip inside the castle without drawing attention, get close enough to the records and the death warrants, and adjust them—not to erase them, but to change them just enough to make the execution something we can work with and ultimately break.

Tomas breaks my thoughts. "We'll need the right seals, and someone inside who won't hesitate."

"You'll have them," I say. "Whatever you need, I'll get it."

He studies me for a moment, maybe gauging whether I'm ready to move after the way he found me earlier. I give him nothing but sure looks. Ava's counting on me, and that's all that matters.

We gather around the cracked mosaic in the center of the floor, the faded pattern of blue and gold now our map table. I lay out what little we can risk speaking openly, and the rest we leave unsaid, each of us filling in the blanks in our own way.

As the meeting breaks, I stand with Tomas, Matius, Luis, and Martin, possibly for the last time.

Tomas steps forward. "You've carried us this far. We will always remember you as our leader."

Matius nods, his expression hard. "There's no one else we'd follow."

Luis looks me in the eye. "Your death will be an honorable one, Luca."

Martin places a firm hand on my shoulder. "We've been through hell together. It won't be the same without you."

I swallow hard. "After I'm gone, and only once you're sure I'm gone, you'll need to find a letter I'll leave here." I point toward a narrow crack in the far wall, nearly hidden by shadows. "It'll be tucked right there."

They don't argue or try to stop me. We all know the road ahead doesn't guarantee a return.

With a final nod, they hit the streets, each taking their place in the fight to come. I stay behind for a moment, my hand on the folded parchment.

The grief hasn't gone, but it's hardened into resolve. If Ava can fight from inside those walls, I can fight from out here, and I would die to save her. Tomorrow at dawn, I'll be where I need to be, waiting in the shadows by the Tagus, ready for whatever may come.

2 8

---

# HE'S NOT HERE

### *AVA*

THE BELL TOWER STRIKES MIDNIGHT, the deep chime echoing off damp stone. When it fades, only the slow drip of water and the thud of my own pulse remain. Down here, time is measured only by those distant bells. In the pressing dark, it's impossible to tell one hour from the next otherwise.

Footsteps scrape on the stairwell. Not the slow, lazy shuffle of the usual guard who drops my food. These are purposeful, almost eager. My stomach knots before I even see him.

The torchlight flares in the doorway. A tall, broad-shouldered man with a smirk that makes my skin crawl steps into view.

"Couldn't sleep?" he asks, his voice dripping with false sympathy. "Thought I'd come and give you the good news."

I keep my face still, even though my heart kicks faster. "And what news would that be?"

He leans against the bars like we're sharing a joke. "I know how you're going to die at dawn. Thought you might like to picture it while you've got the time. It'll be ugly."

I brace myself, already certain of the words he's about to say. *Burned at the stake.* I've imagined the flames too many times already, the heat, the screaming....

"We're throwing you in the river," he says instead, smiling wider when he sees my confusion.

For a split second, I'm frozen. Then the fear shifts, now laced with a jolt of relief so strong it almost makes me dizzy. The plan worked, and Luca accomplished his mission. My death warrant is exactly what I'd hoped for.

I force myself to take a deep breath, but my mind is racing. Being thrown in the river means I might be able to return home to 2025.

*Or it could mean I drown.*

The guard tilts his head. "Not so tough now, are you?" He taps the bars with his knuckles, then turns and disappears up the stairs, taking the torchlight with him.

Darkness swallows me again. I try to picture the moment, dawn light over the water, hands shoving me from behind, the cold closing over my head.

I've told myself I'm ready, and that I'd rather take this chance than burn or be hung, but now, as reality settles in, I'm not sure. If I drown, I'll never see Luca or my family again.

But if it works, I'll wash up in my own time, and everything here will be over.

* * *

THE DUNGEON DOOR CRASHES OPEN. A BREEZE RUSHES IN, SMELLING faintly of horses. I feel as though I may be ill, as the guard from earlier, my messenger of doom, grins at me like a wolf that's already tasted his kill.

"Time to go, heretic," he says, his voice brimming with triumph.

They yank me up, and my legs are so stiff from sitting too long on stone that each step is a stumble, each breath painful in my lungs.

The hallway is lined with shadows, the sconces barely throwing enough light to guide our way. I catch a glance through the barred windows as we pass. It's still dark out there, but not for much longer.

Outside, the sky is a deep, cloudless gray. A wagon waits in the courtyard, its wheels caked with mud. I feel weak as the guards push me forward. Suddenly, nausea ripples through my stomach, and I stop, bending over to vomit onto the stone street.

The guards don't seem to notice or care. They shove me roughly into the back of the wagon. The boards creak beneath me, heavy with damp wood rot. The smell hits me immediately, stale and suffocating.

My heart hammers so loud I'm sure the men outside can hear it. My plan worked—at least, the part where they decided on the river instead of fire. Luca pulled it off somehow. But now, faced with the reality of it, I can't stop imagining what will happen if the rest of the plan fails.

If the river doesn't spit me out in 2025.

If I just sink.

If my lungs fill with icy water, and I'm lost forever.

The wagon lurches forward. My knees knock together as we roll over uneven ground, every bump jarring through my bones.

I move toward the tiny barred window in the side panel, pressing my face close to the iron. My breath fogs in the chilled morning air. The streets we pass are empty. No curious villagers, no onlookers waiting to jeer. It's too early, even for that. I search desperately for a familiar face, but there's nothing and no one.

The wagon groans as it turns, the driver shouting at the horses. I fight back tears brought on by the creeping certainty that I am completely alone.

I dig my fingers into the splintered wood of the bench as we rattle over a bump, the boards drumming under the wheels. The river can't be far now.

When we reach the Tagus, the driver stops his team. The guards drag me from the wagon. My boots scrape against the bridge, the sound drowned beneath the low roar of voices ahead. The river glints silver in the early light.

A crowd waits at the bank, their faces pale in the dawn. Tomas, Matius, Luis, Martin, and even Catalina follow me with their eyes as the guards march me forward. No one speaks. Catalina's chin trembles, and tears slip silently down her cheeks.

I want to call out to her, to any of them, but my throat is too tight to make a sound.

I dart my eyes over the sea of faces, desperate for one. Luca. He has to be here. I scan again, faster, harder, willing him to appear from the mass of bodies. Nothing.

My stomach turns to stone.

He must have been caught. Maybe they locked him up for stabbing the guard. Maybe they killed him. The thought slices through me so sharply, I almost fall on my face.

Hot tears blur the edges of the world. I can't stop them. The guards force me closer to the edge. My knees go weak when I hear the rush of water below.

One yanks me to a stop. The other takes my wrists and jerks them forward. Rope scrapes across my skin as they bind them too tight. Then they crouch and seize my ankles. The hemp coils around, rough and unyielding, biting into my skin. The knot is brutal, final.

A fresh wave of panic rips through me. This is different. I thought I'd be able to swim. I thought that if my plan worked, I'd wash up in the moat in 2025, coughing up water, but alive. But with my wrists and ankles tied, I can't move. I can't fight the water in the moat or the Tagus River if I'm bound.

The guards' hands are iron on my arms, steering me toward the river's edge. Every step feels like it takes me further from air, from light, from anything that could save me.

I drag my gaze back to the crowd one last time, still hoping, still praying to see Luca's face. The plan was to let me go back to my time, but I had hoped to at least shout a goodbye to Luca as I fell.

He's not here.

The water of the Tagus churns below, dark and restless, catching the faint light of dawn in broken shards. The current's voice is a low growl beneath the screams, tugging at the edge of my thoughts.

A sob tears out of me, raw and shaking. My chest feels too small for air.

The water rushes louder now. The guards step to the edge, and I stumble forward with them. My knees almost buckle. One of the guards mutters something I can't hear over the blood pounding in my ears. Their hands shove against my back.

They lift me onto the edge of the bridge, and the river leaps toward me.

Out of the corner of my eye, I catch movement—someone breaking from the shadows and running hard. A figure launches off the bank the same instant my body tips forward into the air.

The plunge knocks the breath from me. The water is colder than I imagined, shocking, stabbing into my skin like a thousand needles. It closes over my head, sealing me in. My lungs scream for air. The ropes at my wrists keep my arms pinned and useless.

Panic tears through me. My body jerks, twists, but I only sink deeper. The current yanks at me, spinning me sideways. My chest burns. I open my mouth in a silent cry and taste the grit of the river.

Hands grab me, rough and urgent. A knife slices the rope from my wrists. I claw upward, trying to kick, but my ankles are still bound.

I feel a tug on my legs, hands around me holding me still, and then rope fibers parting.

I kick free, upward, toward the surface, but my head feels light and hollow. My vision blurs and narrows.

The river swallows the last of the light, and everything goes black.

## 29

# HOME

### *LUCA*

WATER CLOSES IN AROUND ME, dark and crushing. My lungs burn, my muscles scream, but I push harder, searching through the murky gloom. A faint, shimmering light appears ahead, breaking through the cold blackness like a beacon. I reach for it, and for her.

I close my fingers around Ava's arm. She's limp, heavy in the river. I pull with everything I have, fighting the relentless current. The ropes around her ankles are cut, but still bind her, slowing us both. I wrench them free, my heart pounding, my lungs desperate for air.

Finally, the light grows brighter and warmer, as we reach the surface. I kick upward, pulling Ava with me until we break through the water. I cough and sputter, dragging her onto the muddy bank. My arms shake as I roll her onto her side, my fingers pressing her ribs, willing her to breathe.

Her chest rises and falls unevenly. Then, a choking, gasp. Water sputters from her mouth, and at last, she inhales a full breath. Relief crashes over me like a wave. She coughs again, trembling, then opens her eyes.

I glance around, scanning the world beyond the river. This place looks nothing like anything I've ever seen. Large tents, colorful banners fluttering in the breeze. Wooden stalls closed for the night, and behind them, a tall castle gate that looks like a painting, too perfect, too new.

Confusion and wonder flood me. I want to ask many questions, but Ava looks too weak to speak.

Eventually, her gaze finds mine, and she pushes herself upright, sobbing tears of joy, bouncing on the balls of her feet like a child. "We're... we're back," she says, her voice shaky. "We're home. It's the Renaissance Festival—in 2025."

I stare at her, stunned. "Festival? Is this *your* '2025'?"

She laughs through her tears, a sound so beautiful I almost forget the terror we just escaped. "It's the future, Luca. We made it. You're safe. We're both safe!"

For a moment, the strange world around me fades. I don't care if it's 2025, 1492 or any time in between. I'm just glad we are together.

This odd castle, this festival, none of it matters right now. All that matters is that Ava is alive, and for the first time in what feels like forever, I believe all has worked out for the best.

Ava wraps her arms around me tightly, and I hold her as if I'll never let go. "We're here," she whispers. "We made it."

I brush the damp hair from her face, amazed by the warmth and life returning to her. "But... what is this place? What festival?"

She leans back just enough to smile, wiping tears from her cheeks. "It's called a Renaissance Festival. People dress up like it's the time you're from, but it's just pretend. A celebration, a way to remember history, have fun, and learn."

I study the bright tents, the painted signs, and the castle walls behind us. "Pretend? People do this for fun?"

Ava laughs, a sound full of wonder. "Yes. But it's also a place where I teach. Come with me."

She takes my hand and leads me through the quiet stalls to a small booth adorned with old maps, books, and pictures. "This is my booth," she says proudly. "I teach here, history, especially about the era in which you lived."

I study the pictures of castles with towering walls and battlements sharp against the sky. One looks like the Alcázar de Toledo, but it seems changed, newer somehow—different from the palace I remember. Five hundred years have altered it, yet its strength remains. It feels both familiar and strange.

"The language you speak isn't quite the same as the modern language. You'll need to relearn Spanish, and you'll probably want to learn English too."

I nod, the thought of learning new languages overwhelming but exciting.

She squeezes my hand. "You saved me, Luca. I don't know how to thank you."

I shake my head, bringing her closer. "I couldn't let you drown. When I saw you thrown into the water, I didn't hesitate. I jumped in, cut the ropes. I made sure you lived."

"You risked everything for me. Again."

I lean down and kiss her. She meets me halfway, her hands resting lightly on my chest. When we finally part, she looks up at me. "We're together," she says. "That's all that matters."

I smile, feeling something I never thought I'd feel again: hope.

She steps away just a little and scans the booth. "Maybe my bag is still here."

She kneels quickly, reaching behind a loose wooden panel on the side of the booth. Her fingers find a small carved notch where she's tucked the key. She unlocks the cabinet door and reaches inside, retrieving a small leather purse and a sleek black rectangle that glows faintly in the dark.

"What is that?" I ask, staring at the flat object.

She smiles, brushing dirt from her hands. "That's my phone, like I spoke of before. It lets me talk to people far away. I can call my parents and my sister. I'm going to speak with them as soon as we get back to my apartment and let them know I'm all right."

"Apartment?" I echo, the word unfamiliar.

She nods. "It's where I live. Like a small house, but inside a big building."

I study her face, amazed by how calm she is, how this world is so natural to her. "And… your parents and sister? They are waiting for you?"

"Yes," she says, her eyes shining. "They must be so worried. I wonder how much time has passed."

Ava picks up the black box once again, and it lights up like magic in the dimly lit space. She stares at it, her expression filled with wonder. "It's amazing," she says softly. "Only a few hours have passed here… but back in 1492, weeks went by."

She stands, comfort and peace settling over her face. "Come on. I'll show you my car."

I follow her outside the gates, stepping carefully over loose stones and discarded parchment fluttering in the cool night breeze. The moonlight glints off a sleek metal shape parked nearby.

"That's a car?" I ask, still bewildered by everything.

She laughs. "Yeah, a car. It's how we get around here."

I run my hand over the smooth surface, surprised at how different it is from the horses and carts I know. "Is it fast?"

"It will seem very fast at first, and it'll take some getting used to," she says, opening the door for me. "But right now, we just need to get home."

The car rumbles to life with a growl. We rapidly move away from the empty festival grounds, the night sky stretching wide above us.

"It's so much faster than a horse and cart," I say, amazed by the speed and smoothness of the ride.

As we drive, Ava talks about the world and how it's changed. She talks about how people live, work, and connect. I listen, trying to soak it all in, my mind racing.

The city lights grow nearer, glowing like a cluster of tiny stars brought down to earth, so bright and shiny, unlike the torchlight I know from my time. Signs light up and flash in a riot of colors–red, blue, green, and yellow–painting the night in wild strokes of light. The streets hum with the roar of machinery, dozens of cars weaving past each other like a swarm of bees.

I watch her control her car, her hands on the wheel, her eyes sharp. How does she do it? So many cars, so many people, all moving at once, and she never flinches. It's like she's part of the road itself, flowing smoothly through the chaos. I'm always impressed by her, so remarkably fearless.

As we step into Ava's home, warm and buzzing with life, the hum of machines I don't understand fills the air. Glass and steel are everywhere. There's rich fabric on couches, and inexplicably glowing rectangles stacked like magic stones.

I stand still for a moment, overwhelmed by the new languages I must learn, the foreign sounds and ways of this time, and the inventions that seem like sorcery. My mind swirls with confusion and awe, but above it all, excitement reigns.

I left behind a world filled with sorrow, war, fear, and endless nights haunted by loss. I left behind pain I thought would follow me forever.

Ava leads me to the washroom, where we rinse away the grime and cold of the river. The hot water shooting out of the wall is an unusual kind of magic fountain. I never knew such comfort existed.

Afterward, she pulls something from a drawer and hands it to me. "Sweatpants and a hoodie," she says with a smile. I slip into them, and the softness, the weightlessness, the ease envelopes me. I close my eyes and say, almost laughing, "These are so comfortable, I might go mad."

She giggles, the sound light and pure.

Later, after she's settled onto the couch, having just called her family and spoken English with them on that bizarre little device she calls a phone, I look at her and say, "There's something I need to tell you."

Ava looks up at me, her eyes bright with curiosity. "What is it?" she asks, leaning forward.

"In the bathhouse, behind the wall, I left a coded message for my friends so they'd know that if I never return, if my body never washes up on the shore of the Tagus, it means I have gone forward, into the future. That I have escaped death and am with you, somewhere far away."

She smiles, her expression softening with something like awe and relief. "That was so thoughtful and brave of you, Luca. I can't even begin to tell you how grateful I am," she says. "You risked everything jumping into that river. You saved me. Twice. I don't know how to thank you."

I swallow the lump in my throat, feeling a warmth spread through my chest. "Ava, you saved me, too," I say quietly. "You rescued me from darkness. I never imagined a life beyond those city walls of burning fear. But here, with you, I have a chance at happiness."

I pull her close, and my lips meet hers. She melts into the kiss, and when we part, I look into her eyes and know this is where I belong.

Home isn't bound by place or era. With Ava, I am home, and I will hold on to that forever.

# 30

# TOGETHER

## *AVA*

LIFE FEELS ALMOST NORMAL AGAIN. It's strange how quickly my days have slipped back into a rhythm, as if the weeks I spent in the fifteenth century were just a vivid dream I finally woke from.

Every morning, our apartment smells like fresh coffee, and I wake to Luca singing as he makes us breakfast. He kisses me goodbye, and I drive to work.

As I stand in front of my class, a marker in my hand, writing dates on the board, the murmur of students flipping through notebooks is comforting. I'd missed the way history opens up in front of curious minds, missed the debates and half-formed theories that turn into "aha" moments. My voice feels stronger now when I lecture, like surviving everything I did has somehow settled me more firmly into myself.

After class, I walk across the green to meet my sister Eden for lunch. The campus smells faintly of rain, the grass still wet from last night's storm. She's already at our favorite cafe, waving from the corner table.

She doesn't know what happened. None of my family members do. For them, no time passed. One day I was here, and the next I was still here. There was no gap for them to notice, and no missing weeks to explain.

But for me, every hug feels more precious. I hold my sister a little longer than necessary when I greet her, and I listen more intently when she tells me about her career and the new guy she's seeing.

Lunch is fun. We share stories, and tease each other the way we always have. It's so normal, it almost makes my chest ache. When we part, I promise to come by for Sunday dinner, and she rolls her eyes, saying I'd better not cancel this time.

The walk home is short. My apartment building looms warm and familiar, and when I open the door, the scent of something garlicky hits me. Luca's in the kitchen, his sleeves rolled up, stirring a pan on the stove. He glances up, and the gorgeous smile that spreads across his face reminds me of how lucky I am.

He asks about my day and tells me about the errands he ran. I set the table while he talks, our movements weaving together like we've been doing this for years instead of months. I'm no longer waiting for the ground to give way under my feet. Life is wonderful, and I'm here to live it.

Luca takes to modern Spanish quickly. His accent softens in just a few weeks, and his English comes much faster than I expected.

"You are... beautiful," he says one morning while flipping pancakes. His English is deliberate, careful, but his eyes are warm and teasing.

I smirk. "You learned that day one."

"Yes," he admits, grinning. "But I like to practice."

Life with him is full in a way I didn't think possible. We still talk about Toledo sometimes. We talk about narrow streets and candlelit nights, about the danger and fear, but it's not as heavy anymore. When the memories edge toward the ache of grief, we sit together on the couch, holding one another, speaking of the painful memories aloud until the tension eases.

I've never been in a relationship with someone who doesn't try to change the subject when things get difficult before. Luca is here now, kind, patient, and willing to meet me where I am, even when that means stumbling through a language that isn't his own.

A few days ago, Luca came home with a guitar. It was secondhand, its wood worn smooth from someone else's fingers, but it sang under his touch. "Music," he told me in Spanish, "is another way to keep the heart healthy."

He's been composing since then, slow melodies that rise and fall like the old songs he used to hum in Toledo. I stir sauce on the stove while he plays. Before long, we're singing together, my voice harmonizing with his.

We don't need grand declarations every day. Sometimes, it's enough that he plays, I sing, and the scent of garlic and bread fills the apartment while the world hums quietly outside.

Amid the calm of our routine, Luca and I found ourselves drawn back to the past in a new way. Between the ordinary rhythms of cooking, laughter, and quiet evenings, we carved out time to dive into dusty archives and faded documents, searching for traces of the lives we once knew. What began as a personal quest to find fragments of our friends and loved ones soon grew into something more: a shared mission to breathe life into history.

The dining table is a mess with papers, old books, scanned manuscripts spread everywhere, like a storm passed through. My laptop's glow pools over Luca's face as he studies a faded page from an archive. The smell of coffee hangs in the air, mingling with the faint tang of the old leather-bound volumes we borrowed from the university collection.

We've been at this for nearly a year now, working in pockets of time between classes, concerts, and everyday life. Some days we find nothing at all. Other days, we find a breadcrumb, one small, fragile thread connecting us back to the people we left in Toledo.

The first one came in the spring. Luca spotted a merchant record from Valencia. *Tomas de Morales* lived until 1516 and owned three ships. We celebrated with wine that night, imagining him sailing to far-off ports, still chasing adventure.

Weeks later, on a rainy afternoon, I found Samira in the records of

Cordoba, listed as *Samira bint Khalid,* a midwife who lived until 1534. Luca smiled for a long time after that, saying midwifery suited her perfectly. I could almost hear her voice again.

Summer brought frustration. For months, nothing surfaced. We scoured Portuguese archives, church ledgers, tax rolls. Finally, in late August, my eyes caught a familiar name—*Luis de la Vega*, Lisbon. A master cartographer. Of course. I grinned through tears, remembering his love of maps.

Martin's name appeared in winter. A tiny entry in a wedding record in Seville—married, four children, gone in 1522. My fingers lingered on his name.

We haven't found the others. Maybe they changed their names, or maybe the records are gone. We don't speak about the darker possibilities aloud.

I close my laptop and lean into Luca's side. "At least we know some of them made it."

He wraps his arm around me. "And we'll keep looking."

We continue searching, month after month, between classes, concerts, and lazy Sunday mornings, following the trail of our friends one clue at a time.

Sometimes the work leaves us quiet, thoughtful. Other times it sparks hours of conversation about the lives they built after we left. Somewhere in the middle of it all, a new idea takes root. If we can bring the past to life for ourselves, maybe we can do it for others too.

It starts as a little joke between us. Luca leans back in his chair, grinning. "You know, I could make a living pretending I still haven't left the fifteenth century."

I laugh, but by the next week, we're standing in the brightly lit gymnasium of an elementary school, both of us grinning like we've been caught doing something slightly ridiculous. A banner over the stage reads *History Week!* in uneven letters drawn by kids.

Luca's in a tunic I stitched together from thrift store finds, the fabric draping just so, a leather belt cinched at his waist. The kids' eyes go wide the second he steps out, carrying his lute like it's the most normal thing in the world.

"Good morning," he says in slow, careful English, still carrying that warm lilt of Spanish from his time. "I am Luca, from the city of Toledo. The year is 1492, or at least it was, until I walked into your school today."

A ripple of laughter moves through the audience. He's in his element, spinning stories about cobblestone streets, crowded markets, and the smell of bread baking in outdoor ovens.

When he sings, the room falls into a hush. The notes are simple, pure, and the sound of the lute threads through the air like golden light. The kids don't take their eyes off him.

When it's my turn, I pull up a slideshow of buildings from Luca's time, arches and spires, fortress walls and winding alleyways. "Luca actually walked through these streets," I tell them. "This was home for him. And yes—he had to dodge goats more often than people."

The kids giggle. I tell them about Queen Isabella and King Ferdinand, about the artists and thinkers of the age, weaving in Luca's anecdotes.

Afterward, the kids swarm us. They ask if he's *really* from the past, if he's seen a dragon, if he knows any knights. Luca takes it all in stride, answering with twinkling eyes, never breaking character.

On the drive home, he sits back in the passenger seat, still in his tunic. "They believed me," he says, grinning.

"They wanted to believe you," I reply. "And maybe that's the best kind of history, when it feels like magic."

His hand finds mine, warm and familiar. "Then let's keep making magic."

We do. We travel to school after school, town after town, telling stories, playing music, reminding kids that history isn't just in books. It's alive, and sometimes, if you're very lucky, it walks right into your life.

The sun is low when we finally make it home, still grinning from the children's laughter, and their endless questions about "what it's like to be from the past." Luca tosses his bag on the couch, his eyes warm and soft when they meet mine.

I walk into the kitchen, set down my notes, and feel him behind me before I hear his footsteps. His arms slide around my waist, his chin settling on my shoulder.

"You're my favorite part of this century," he says.

I turn, looking up at him, and he kisses me. When we break apart, he sweeps his thumb across my cheek. "Do you ever think about how lucky we were to find each other?"

"Every day," I whisper. "And I'll keep thinking about it for the rest of my life."

"Was it worth it? Going through time and the horrors of the Inquisition to find me?" he asks.

"Of course. I would return to you in every lifetime, in any era, no matter the cost. What about you? Is it worth it to learn new languages and a completely new way of life to be with me?"

"Yes," he says without hesitation. "Because in every century I've known, people chase knowledge, chase power, chase survival. I only ever wanted to chase you."

I laugh, a little breathless, and shake my head. "You make it sound like I was running."

"You were," he says, smiling. "Through centuries, through rivers, across oceans, and somehow, we ended up here. Together."

# ALSO BY ID JOHNSON

**Stand Alone Titles**

All I Want for Christmas is Pooch

*(sweet contemporary romance)*

Christmas Memory

*(sweet contemporary romance)*

Meet Cute Me Under the Mistletoe

*(sweet contemporary romance)*

The Doll Maker's Daughter at Christmas

*(clean romance/historical)*

Pretty Little Monster

*(young adult/suspense)*

The Journey to Normal: Our Family's Life with Autism *(nonfiction)*

Found by the Alpha (fantasy romance)

**Love Throughout Time**

*(time travel romance)*

Back to Titanic

Back to Gettysburg

Back to Bunker Hill

Back to the Highlands

Back to Port Royal

Back to the Inquisition

Back to Salem (Oct 2025)

Back to Plymouth (Nov 2025)

Back to Whitechapel (Dec 2025)

Back to the Old West (Jan 2026)

Back to the Ton (Feb 2026)

Back to the Crown (March 2026)

Back to Pompeii (April 2026)

**Silverwood Academy**

*(paranormal romance)*

Vampire Hunter

World Builder

Realm Jumper

**Celestial Springs**

*(psychological thriller/literary fiction/women's fiction)*

<u>Beneath the Inconstant Moon</u>

<u>The First Mrs. Edwards</u>

<u>Leaving Ginny</u>

**The Motherhood**

*(dystopian romance)*

<u>Rain's Rebellion</u>

<u>Rain's Run</u>

<u>Rain's Return</u>

**Ashes and Rose Petals**

*(contemporary romance/retelling of Romeo and Juliet and Cinderella)*

<u>Girl in the Attic</u>

<u>Girl From the Tomb</u>

<u>Girl On the Beach</u>

**Nashville Country Dreams**

*(contemporary romance)*

<u>Meant to Marry Me</u>

Lead Me Home

You Are the Reason

**Forever Love series**

*(clean romance/historical)*

Cordia's Will: A Civil War Story of Love and Loss

Cordia's Hope: A Story of Love on the Frontier

**The Clandestine Saga series**

*(paranormal romance)*

Transformation

Resurrection

Repercussion

Absolution

Illumination

Destruction

Annihilation

Obliteration

Termination

**A Vampire Hunter's Tale (based on The Clandestine Saga)**

*(paranormal/alternate history)*

Aaron

Jamie

Elliott

Christian

**The Chronicles of Cassidy (based on The Clandestine Saga)**

*(young adult paranormal)*

So You Think Your Sister's a Vampire Hunter?

Who Wants to Be a Vampire Hunter?

How Not to Be a Vampire Hunter

My Life As a Teenage Vampire Hunter

Vampire Hunting Isn't for Morons

Vampires Bite and Other Life Lessons

Gone Guardian

Death Does Not Become Her

**Blood of the Vampire Hunter (based on The Clandestine Saga)**

*(paranormal romance)*

Night Slayer

Shadow Stalker

Queen Catcher

Mother Hunter

Father Finder

**Ghosts of Southampton series**

*(historical romance)*

Prelude

Titanic

Residuum

Lusitania

**Heartwarming Holidays Sweet Romance series**

*(Christian/clean romance)*

Melody's Christmas

Christmas Cocoa

Winter Woods

Waiting On Love

Shamrock Hearts

A Blossoming Spring Romance

Firecracker!

Falling in Love

Thankful for You

Melody's Christmas Wedding

The New Year's Date

**Charles Town Brides (based on Heartwarming Holidays Sweet Romance)**

*(Christian/clean romance)*

From This Moment

Can't Help Falling in Love

It's Your Love

When You Say Nothing At All

My Girl

Unchained Melody

I Only Have Eyes For You

At Last

The Very Thought of You

**Reaper's Hollow**

*(paranormal/urban fantasy)*

Ruin's Lot

Ruin's Promise

Ruin's Legacy

**When Kings Collide**

*(steamy historical romance)*

Princess of Silence

Princess of Hearts

**Collections**

Ghosts of Southampton Books 0-2

Reaper's Hollow Books 1-3

The Clandestine Saga Books 1-3

The Chronicles of Cassidy Books 1-4

Celestial Springs Collection

Heartwarming Holidays Sweet Romance Books 1-3

Heartwarming Holidays Sweet Romance Books 4-7

Websites: https://books2read.com/ap/xX7ZD8/ID-Johnson

For updates, visit www.authoridjohnson.blogspot.com

Follow on Twitter @authoridjohnson

Find me on Facebook at www.facebook.com/IDJohnsonAuthor

Instagram: @authoridjohnson

Follow me on Bookbub: https://www.bookbub.com/authors/id-johnson